CANDLELIGHT REGENCY SPECIAL

CANDLELIGHT REGENCIES

MANSION FOR A LADY

Cilla Whitmore

Published by
Dell Publishing Co., Inc.
1 Dag Hammarskjold Plaza
New York, New York 10017

Dell ® TM 681510, Dell Publishing Co., Inc.

ISBN: 0-440-16097-9

Printed in the United States of America
First printing—October 1980

CHAPTER I

"Vitruvius? Vitruvius! What has Vitruvius to say to anything?" The smartly dressed young lady pointed a finger of scorn at the drawings spread out upon the young man's drawing table.

The look of weary long-suffering that appeared upon Mr. David Crenshaw's face bespoke a conflict that had not just begun. With a tone of exaggerated patience, he turned about on his high stool and peered at her over his spectacles.

"My dear Miss Thorpe, the venerable Vitruvius just happens to be the Father of Architecture. I shall be very pleased if you would be so kind as to mind your own business and allow me to proceed with my work."

"My dear Mr. Crenshaw, you need not take that superior attitude with me! I know precisely who the venerable Vitruvius is, and he is more the great-great-great-grandfather of architecture. There have been, since his day, a fair number of other practitioners in the field who have managed to improve upon the ancient gentleman's designs. It seems to me that it is an imposition upon the client to attempt to foist such ancient trumpery upon him. It is for the Duke of Roxbury, is it not?"

"What if it is? His grace has specified a dignified structure, and what could be more dignified than a design that is tried and true? What could be more respectable than a work from the master, Vitruvius?"

"That is nonsensical to a degree!" she shot back. "It is a dwelling his grace is in want of, not a temple to worship in. What you are proposing in that sketch is a Roman basilica, by heaven! Pray, how does one go about living in a Roman basilica?"

"For God's sake, Miranda, must you have a say in every plan, every sketch, every design that is laid out in this office? I pray you will not take an affront when I point out to you that this is a firm of architects—a firm, I must point out, that is the proprietorship of your uncle. If you have any complaint to make of my work, I suggest you take it directly to Mr. Thorpe. I am but carrying out his instructions as he has received them from the duke."

"That does not, of necessity, make it a good choice or even a correct one, David. Architecture is a matter of taste. Vitruvius is neither oracle nor scripture. He was designing for the Romans, who lived upon the sunny shores of the Mediterranean Sea. This, my good friend, is England, where it can be rather damp and chilly. The Romans may have conquered England, but I will wager it was

6

our ungracious weather that sent them back to Italy. Indeed, we may have the renowned fogs of London to thank for the fact that we are not speaking Latin this very day!"

"Oh, Miranda, why do you go on like that? Of course, I shall not be following Vitruvius to the very letter and line. Here, look you! There is provision for fireplaces and there are walls between the pillars. Naturally, they have got to be true pillars and not reliefs if we are to support the roof with them, you understand."

"Fireplaces in a Roman villa? It is to laugh!" Miranda burst out into mocking laughter. "What you have got there, Mr. Crenshaw, is a bastardized mongrel of a creation. Just imagine—chimney stacks poking through the dome of the Pantheon!"

This time her laugh was truly filled with humor, and Mr. Crenshaw had to smile at the notion, too.

But he shook his head. "Miranda, you may say what you will, but the plan is fixed. Mr. Thorpe's instructions were quite clear to me and I am carrying them out. That, my girl, is precisely what I am paid to do. Now, why do you not go out to the shops and leave me to my work? After all, it is hardly a subject to concern females."

"Oh, you can be insufferable without even trying, Mr. Crenshaw," she retaliated. "If you continue with that monstrosity, I am going to speak with my uncle. It is a disgrace to the firm, and to his grace, that such a poor effort should be submitted. Good day to you, sir!" She tossed her head and walked out of the office, nose high in the air.

Mr. Crenshaw let out a great sigh and shook his head as he turned back to the table. Before he could lift up his straightedge and pencil, George Piper, at the next table, made a show of peering at him and exclaimed, "Now then, David my boy, that is no way to get on with your master's ward. You will never rise to be a proper partner in this enterprise, I assure you."

"Oh, be still, Piper! If that is your idea of a wife, welcome to her. She knows everything that is to be known about architecture—she thinks! I say heaven defend me from all manner of blue-stockings, and may it make a special effort with regard to young ladies who deem themselves versed in the lore of architecture. A more unappealing wife I cannot imagine."

"Let it not be a worry to you, old chap. I do not see that she is likely to set her cap for you."

"Oh, go back to your work. Piper, you have got a big mouth."

The young man opened his mouth wide, then grinned. Mr. Crenshaw snatched up his little block of caoutchouc and threw it at his colleague. The bit of rubber hit Mr. Piper's drawing table and bounced off into a corner of the office as though it were a living thing.

"Here now!" expostulated Mr. Piper. "Let us not be tossing our lead-eaters about, especially you! I venture to say that you are forever rubbing out your mistakes and would be unable to draw without it."

"Is that a fact? Then pray inform me, who was it that put in a request to Mr. Thorpe for a new supply of erasers? Piper, I had quite enough from Miss Thorpe. I have no wish to get into a debate with you, sir. Get you back to work or I shall have a word or two with Mr. Thorpe about a dilatory hireling. But first pick up my rubber and return it to me."

"The devil I shall! It was you who put it there!"

"Piper, I am fast losing patience with you! Pick up that eraser!"

"Never, sir!"

"Oh, Piper," said Mr. Crenshaw as he eased himself down from his stool and proceeded to the corner for the errant eraser. "I shall not forget this! You will see."

"Look you, Crenshaw, it is never the proper thing to throw things at a chap. Now, if you were any sort of fellow, you'd have . . ."

"Uncle Sylvester, is this a firm of responsible architects or is it not?" Miranda demanded as she strode through the door of Mr. Sylvester Thorpe, Master Architect, offices situated in Upper Parliament Street, Nottingham.

He regarded his niece for a moment, the expression of exasperation on his face akin to what a few moments before had twisted Mr. Crenshaw's features. There was great resignation in his manner as he put down the copy of the London *Times* he had been perusing and regarded Miranda from behind his tiny spectacles. Finally he responded.

"Miranda, my pet, can you not find something more useful to do at the moment? Truly, an architect's place of business is not a very proper place to find a charming young lady of four-and-twenty. I mean to say, my dear, that for all your brilliance, this is a man's business, and, as you are my niece for whom I would do all in my power, I say, why do you not take advantage and go out with your aunt? I am sure there are things you can shop for. There must be! Hardly a day goes by but my Martha discovers something that she is in dire need of and directly is off to the shops. My dear, is not there anything you need?" he asked plaintively.

"Uncle Sylvester, I am on to you and it will not wash," Miranda replied. "We have been at this business before. Do not think to put me off with allusions to my age. If I remain upon the shelf, it will be only because there is no gentleman fated for me—"

"Um, ye-es. Fated is the precise word," he said dryly.

Miranda smiled. "There it is. You just wish to get me off your hands. Admit it."

"Never, my dear, for it is not true. You have a

home with me forever, if that is truly what you wish. And that is precisely the point—a home, not an office. When you are about, my young men do nothing but moon and scribble nonsense when they ought to be laying out the work that I have assigned to them. To make matters worse, you, my dear, go about criticizing all that is done in this office and from very little knowledge, I assure you—"

"It is not fair of you to say so, Uncle Sylvester," protested Miranda, falling into a chair beside his desk.

Mr. Thorpe raised an eyebrow at that and nodded his head, sadly. "Hmmm, I see that you are intent upon taking up my entire morning. Are you quite sure, my sweet, that your Aunt Martha does not have need of you?"

Miranda brushed his remark aside with an impatient wave of her hand. "Uncle, it is time that we had a serious talk, you and I. I am not about to be put off by you. You know very well that my inability to draw up a set of plans is not any indication of my knowledge of architecture. I venture to say without fear of contradiction that I know as much about your Vitruviuses, your Palladios, your Joneses, and your Wrens as Mr. Crenshaw—and a deal more than Mr. Piper. It is beyond nature that you, my uncle, should deny me, your niece, the chance to build all those great and wonderful edifices that fill my dreams. It is not as though it would cost you a penny. I should be happy to do it out of the great love I bear for architecture!" she proclaimed.

Mr. Thorpe did not look particularly impressed. In fact, he looked even more put upon than before, if possible. He raised his eyes to the heavens and cried, "My blessed saints, is this the burden I am to bear to my dying day? Miranda, we have gone all through this business more times than I care to count. I know how much you love the great old buildings, and I know how much you would like to assist in similar constructions, but the facts of the matter have not changed. You are a female and, therefore, not constituted to go about in the fields and the mud to measure, survey, and advise rough laborers. They would only laugh at you—and well they should. You have not the faintest notion of mortar and brick and woods. You have not the faintest notion of how space is to be allocated to the different rooms. You are constantly questioning the masters, all of them—you who have yet to construct the simplest habitation. Why, you cannot even sketch it! Oh dear, dear, must we go on and on about it as though it were a new and novel debate?"

"Oh, Uncle, I do not take issue with any of those old gentlemen when it comes to building an impregnable fortress of a castle or a great place of worship. I am speaking of a home! What man knows more than a woman about how a home ought to be managed, I ask you? That is a woman's place."

"Indeed, I am devoutly pleased that at last we find a ground of agreement. It is precisely what I wish for you. I wish you to find a home, any home—mine, yours, your husband's, when you have one—so long as you do not settle down here in my office. I say, let women manage the homes that men have built for them, and I challenge you to find a man or a woman who will not agree with that sentiment."

Miranda, a very superior look upon her face, retorted, "And pray, what do you say to my being the first lady architect? One has to make a beginning somewhere."

Mr. Thorpe laughed derisively. "Can you imagine me sending you out into the hinterlands to some old and crusty lord? Can you imagine what he would have to say to me? Just look at you! There is not the first air of an architect about you. Hmmm!" He paused and his eyes lighted up. "Perhaps he might just cotton to the idea and never send you back. I say, Miranda, that just might be the way to get you married off. Yes, and you would not have to trouble that pretty head of yours about boards and planks and the pitch of a roof. Indeed, I shall send you out to the very next wealthy young gentleman who has a mind to build himself a house!"

Miranda, her eyes blazing, leaped from her seat

and exclaimed, "Oh, Uncle Sylvester, there is no talking to you when you are in this nasty humor! I can see it is no manner of use to try to be helpful to you. Very well, I shall go down to London. I venture to predict that there will be a place for me in some architect's office there, especially when I tell him that I had my training under the Thorpes of Nottingham."

Mr. Thorpe's face fell. "Good heavens, girl, surely you do not mean it! Why, I am sure I should never hear the end of it. They would claim that I had thrown you out. Miranda, I beg of you! Think of what your father would say were he alive! You know he would never have countenanced any such action on your part. Now why can you not be a good girl and spend your time with your Aunt Martha? She can put you in touch with any number of eligible gentlemen—and you must admit that, at twenty-four years of age, you have not got all that much time remaining to pick and choose, despite the fact that you have some pretensions to beauty and charm."

A shrewd look came into Miranda's eyes. She regarded her uncle with a speculative look as she resumed her seat.

"Sir, I have a proposition to make to you. You have just given me a idea. Perhaps you are right. Perhaps it would be most unwise for me to go to work to be an architect. But that is not to say that I cannot learn all I can about the profession.

14

Other ladies take up painting and music and other such delights. Unfortunately, these do not delight me. I should much prefer to plan a structure, even if I never live to see the day it rises upon the land."

"I do not see that this makes any sense at all—nor does it get you out of this office, my dearest wish!"

"Oh, Uncle, you know that you do not mean that. You do enjoy having me about. It is just that you do not like it when I become a bother to Piper and Crenshaw. Now, you have been thinking of taking another junior man on—and all you would do with him would be to seat him at a drawing table. Well, I can do that much. I should need but a minimum of instruction, for I have picked up a great deal of the business. You know I have!"

Mr. Thorpe made a face and said, "Still, I do not see this as any sort of proposition. It is all on your side thus far."

"In exchange, I should be quite willing to go about with Aunt Martha every other day and behave like a very proper niece ought to. I should even be willing to entertain gentlemen. Who knows but that I may meet someone who will put all thought of architecture out of my mind?"

Mr. Thorpe grunted. "I doubt that very much—but it sounds to me something less disturbing to the operation of this office than what we now have—and , if ever you are to make a decent marriage, this has got to be the time. It is a desperate remedy, and I am sure I have a very good idea of the tribulation the firm of Thorpe and Brother will suffer. But it is the only chance—a small one I admit—to see you settled in life—"

"I say, Uncle—who was the Thorpe and who was the Brother? You never did say."

A little smile appeared on his lips as he replied, "We never bothered to find out, your father and I. After all, what difference did it make?"

"You would not care to change it to Thorpe and Niece, would you?"

"Miss Thorpe, your first duty as a member of this firm is—Out! Out, I say! Go find yourself a place to work and don't dare show your face on these premises tomorrow. That day you will spend with your aunt as we have agreed. Now, stop bedeviling me and go bother Crenshaw for a bit!"

CHAPTER II

"Anthony Farnsworth, as I live and breath!" cried
Sir Tobias Trimwell as the viscount came into the
taproom of the tiny Robin's Arms. The pub con-
sited of a rough-hewn chamber of oak in which
more than six patrons would have found barely
the space to sit themselves down, not that the
benches along the wall were in the least inviting.
For decoration there was an old longbow hung
upon the wall behind a row of three casks, which
rested on their sides on spindly-legged cradles.
Two deal tables, as rough and rickety as the
benches, served to support the mugs and the el-
bows of any patrons who happened to be partaking of the excellent ale that was served. Sir Toby,
a gentleman of solid weight and proportion, gestured at his lordship with his mug.

Lord Farnsworth nodded to his friend and
neighbor, gestured to the innkeeper, and took a
seat beside the baronet. He let out a sigh and
eased himself back upon the bench as the innkeeper set a mug brimming with yeasty foam
before him. His lordship reached out a languid

hand and raised it to his lips, taking a hearty draft before setting it down again.

"Now what brings you here, Anthony?" asked Sir Toby, his ruddy features split by a wide grin.

"Really, Tobias, why do you insist upon calling me Anthony when I am Tony to all of my other friends?"

Sir Toby stared at Lord Farnsworth for a bit, a look of great surprise on his face. "Why, stab me but you have taken your time to notice! When was the first time you called me Toby, eh?"

"But I have never called you Toby, Tobias!"

"I rest my case," exclaimed Sir Toby triumphantly.

It was obvious that his lordship's mind was not solely concerned with the conversation, because he rubbed his chin as he looked blankly at Sir Toby for a few moments. Then the light dawned and he smiled. "Oh, I say, Toby, I never thought of it. I mean to say Tobias is so dignified and Toby is—well, it is a bit common, you know."

Sir Toby roared with laughter. "Farnsworth, you are a card. Me, dignified? Not on your life! The only time I have ever been addressed as Tobias was when I was a lad and up to my belly-button in hot water with my governor or my master—and the last-mentioned managed to cool me off with a cane at every opportunity. I tell you my days of learning stressed the wrong end o' me, and I prefer not to be reminded of 'em."

"Oh well, in that case I assure you I have no objections to calling you Toby."

Exuding mock gratitude, Sir Toby replied, "I humbly thank you, my lord."

Lord Farnsworth smiled absently at him and nodded.

A look of concern appeared on Sir Toby's face as he lifted his mug only to find it empty. He slammed it down upon the table with a loud crash. Lord Farnsworth gave a start and the innkeeper came running over to pick up the mug and fill it again.

"I say, must you do that?" asked Lord Farnsworth rather petulantly.

"What the devil are you talking about?"

"Really, Tobias—Toby, it is not at all necessary to smash your cup upon the tabletop. There are quieter ways, and pleasanter, to obtain service."

"The trouble with you, Tony old chap, is that you have not been in at the Arms enough. Now if you had visited the place as frequently as I have, you'd know that George, here, doesn't do too well in the hearing department, but he can see his beloved mug dashing itself to smithereens upon the tabletop and he comes arunning."

"Nonsense! I have never had the least trouble with the old fellow. I truly believe that it is not at all necessary and shows a remarkable lack of breeding."

"Hmmm, Tony, I am beginning to believe that

you are not cut out for a life in this quarter of Nottingham. You are too soft. You will never make a go of it. I strongly suggest—now mind you, I do not say this because I have no liking for you. As a matter of fact, I am inordinately proud to call you a friend. Nevertheless, for your own good, I strongly advise you to give it over and pack yourself down to the city."

"Eh? Nottingham?"

"Hardly. That is not a town for the likes of you. I suggest London. By God, if I had your fortune, that is precisely what I would do."

"You would, would you?"

"I would," said Sir Toby with a solemn nod of his head.

"Perhaps then, Sir Toby, you would be kind enough to tell me from whence you would get this great fortune you speak of."

"Well, I have not got it! I refer to the wealth that you inherited. I should imagine that it is something less than when you got it, old chap, pouring it into all those fancy improvements and extraordinary arrangements on your land—"

"Nothing extraordinary about them, my friend. It is just that no one else has put such methods to practice in this district. In any case, they have made my fortune."

Sir Toby laughed. "You mean to say, I believe, that your inheritance allowed you to play about with them—"

"I mean to say nothing of the sort. I have been hard at work putting in those improvements and I had damn little to begin with. The so-called inheritance was not enough to keep body and soul together. My uncle had a strange idea of the extent of the Farnsworth fortune and managed to dissipate nine-tenths of it on the London gaming tables and stage beauties. I assure you there was little enough left of it for me. Fortunately, the house was free of attachments and I was able to raise some money on it. Yesterday I managed to pay it all back and there is quite a sum left over. My man of business was closeted with me all of yesterday and the reckoning was finally completed. Indeed, I am wealthy, old chap, and not yet accustomed to the idea. It has been five years of sweat, argument, and nose to the grindstone. If you have not seen me about much, there's the reason for it. I have been recouping the family fortune. I tell you, the hardest part of it was to get my tenants to follow suit. It was maddening for a bit. They were never able to make up the rent, and I, an utter green-hand, was put to the trouble of showing them how to raise a crop for a profit. ' 'T waren't the way me da said to do!' was their eternal rejoinder every time I made a suggestion."

Sir Toby frowned, then grinned. But Lord Farnsworth was still looking soberly at him and his grin faded. Earnestly, he said, "Tony, are you pulling my leg?"

21

"Of course I am not. Why ever should I?"

"Well, I took you for something of a flat. You had no interest in anything—never joined the lads in a bit of hunting. I mean to say, you are situated right on the edge of Sherwood. It would make sense if you managed to do a bit of poaching every now and again. There is some mighty fine venison disporting itself in those glades, you know."

"Toby, will you never grow up? I should think that a chap of your age would be turning his mind to the more serious purusits of life. Poaching, indeed!"

"When it comes to being serious, I venture to say it will be soon enough. Just because my father was squire was a poor reason for me to become one. I tell you, this being squire *is* serious business. The next thing you know I shall be married and have a house filled with brats. That is even more serious! If I wish to do a bit of poaching, why, bless me! what is the good of being squire if I cannot?"

"The thing of it is that you are supposed to be a pillar of the law of the land. Surely, if the squire commits such offenses against His Majesty's law, why should not everybody?"

"Because they aren't the squire, and I am!" exploded Sir Toby mirthfully.

His lordship regarded him rather sadly and took another swallow from his mug.

"So you had not a feather to fly with before but now you are in fine feather, is that it?" commented Sir Toby.

"Yes, my friend. Now I can take time for myself. The estate can manage for a bit without me."

"Well, if that means we shall be seeing more of you, Tony, it is good news. But, of course, I am sure you will be off to London now."

"What for?"

"Why, to spend a bit of the tin you have worked so hard to collect. Nottingham is hardly the town for excitement."

"Devil take your excitement! I have other things to do with my time."

"I cannot imagine what, except more work on your estate."

"I certainly am not about to let all that I have accomplished go down the drain. Farnsfield is the seat of my family and I expect to continue to reside in it."

"A fine seat that is. It is more a ruin than a great house," pointed out Sir Toby.

Lord Farnsworth looked thoughtful. "Yes, it is a bit of a pile, isn't it?"

He sat in a brown study until Sir Toby demanded with impatience, "Now, what are you thinking?"

"I am thinking that perhaps I ought to do something about it now that I have the money."

"Why, are you not comfortable in it?"

23

"Oh yes, reasonably so, but it strikes me that a wife would not find it at all cozy—"

"A wife?" exclaimed Sir Toby. "If I understand you correctly, you have been at this business morning and night these past—what is it?—five years, I do believe, and the first time you come out for an airing, it is a wife you have on your mind. My lord, forgive the impertinence, but I think you have been working too hard. A wife! Tony, what is wrong with you?"

"I shall tell you what is wrong with me, my fine friend. As you say, I have been hard at this business for a long time, a deal longer than you know. I succeeded to the title when I was twenty-seven years of age. In the years since I have not had time to breathe, much less think of finding me a female to settle down with. You can talk, you can. What are you, Toby, a mere five-and-twenty—"

"I am twenty-eight, and I still think you are off your crock. I have not the least inclination for matrimony, nor is it a matter I am concerned about."

"That is the difference between us then. At two-and-thirty, after years of toiling to make something of this estate of mine, I yearn for the peace and domesticity that a good woman brings to a home."

"Peace and domesticity, is it? Sounds more like a mother than a wife you yearn for, old thing."

"Toby, I do believe you are being rather impertinent!"

"Tony, I am only trying to get you to see things as they truly are. You have buried yourself for so long, your head has become filled with fantastic nonsense. You have worked all these years; now it is time you played about a bit. For heaven's sake, old chap, you are a viscount. Does not that count for anything?"

"Yes, I dare say it does. Surely my wife will be a viscountess," Lord Farnsworth returned with a smile.

Sir Toby shook his head. "I think by the time you are done, you will not only have apartments to let but pockets as well. What woman who wishes to be a viscountess will be satisfied to live in that pile of stone of yours? And, furthermore, she will demand a house in London, and that will set you back a prettier penny than anything you can do to your house here! I swear, if I manage to escape the toils of a female until I reach your age, I shall consider myself safe and be quite content with my life. This is excellent country for all manner of sports, and it is a deuced shame that you are wasting it so."

"You speak like a child, Toby. As it happens, I consider myself to be devoted to a certain party and shall, with all haste, present my suit to her."

"You are? Good heavens, man, is she from the

neighborhood?" Sir Toby was filled at once with surprise and curiosity.

"Frankly, my lad, that is none of your business," returned Lord Farnsworth and he rose up from the table.

"But stay, Tony. Who is the girl? Do I know her?"

"It really does not make the least bit of difference if you do, now does it?"

Sir Toby shook his head slowly. "But you cannot ask her, I do not care who she is. You need a house."

"I pray you will allow me to worry about that. Naturally I would not think of popping the question until I felt I was in a position to receive a wife."

"Then you are going to London?" asked Sir Toby.

"But I have no such intention."

"You have got to get someone in to do the house, don't you?"

Lord Farnsworth scratched his head. "Surely I do not have to go down to the city just to find me a builder. There are houses aplenty about. They could not all have been built by housebuilders from London."

Now it was Sir Toby's turn to scratch his head. "I dare say you are right. There must be some one about. What do you intend having done?"

"How the devil should I know? I have just thought of the idea."

"The devil you say! It was I who gave it to you!" retorted Toby.

"I am sure it hardly matters who thought of it! The thing of it is, how does one go about the business, anyway?"

But Sir Toby was off on another track. "I say, Tony, who the devil can the female be? As far as I know, you have never been about, so who can you have been seeing?"

"How does one go about the business, Toby?"

"Good heavens, man, you just ask her!"

"Whom?" inquired Lord Farnsworth, looking startled.

"Whom?" repeated Sir Toby. "Well, old man, if you don't know, I am sure there are not many who do—and I am not one of them. It is what I have been asking you this past hour. Who is she?"

"My dear Sir Toby, I am speaking of a house-builder. I haven't an inkling as to what you are driveling about."

"This female you have set your heart on, that is what!"

"Are we back to that again? I told you it is none of your business as yet. Now tell me where I am to find a housebuilder, there's a good chap."

Sir Toby looked disappointed. Again he scratched his head. Finally he shrugged his shoulders. "I could make inquiries for you if you would like."

"Where would you begin?"

"If it is not to be from London, I might try in Nottingham."

"Nottingham, of course. I hear that the place is growing by leaps and bounds. I have not been there in a year. Yes, I should start there. Someone is bound to know."

"A year? Ye gods, Tony, I don't know how you can do it. I have not been to *London* in a year and I feel the lack of it!"

"Well, I do not have any time to waste. I thank you for your assistance, Toby. I shall go right down to Nottingham and make inquiries about a housebuilder."

"I'll go down with you. My pair is in need of a good run."

"No, I shall have to wait until next week. There is still a bit of business to keep me close until then. Perhaps we can get together on Tuesday next. I'll let you know exactly. Well, I must be off."

He left the inn and Sir Toby heard him ride off. He shook his head dolefully and muttered, "Poor fish! He is in sad need of help. I think I shall toddle down to Nottingham this afternoon and find him a housebuilder. I am sure he can never do it by himself."

CHAPTER III

Lord Farnsworth had found Sir Toby's presence a bit oppressive. He had entered the inn wearied of soul rather than body and had hoped that at that hour of the morning he could have had the place to himself. He wanted to commune in peace with his ambitions and desires without fear of being interrupted by any calamitous message from his fields. He had put a good part of his life into the estate and, now that it was a blessed sight more than solvent, he was in search of the reward that was due him.

He drove his horse into a canter to make sure that Sir Toby was not following him and, after a half mile of that pace, slowed his horse to a walk.

He had to admit that Sir Toby had spoken a bit of sense. How could he not have thought of it himself? Actually Toby and he had been well met that morning, for it had put him on the right track, and his way was become clearer. He must, as soon as he could get to it, go down to Nottingham and see to a housebuilder. It would have been a crime to have permitted Katherine to have set foot in his domicile in the state that it was.

What a shocking contrast the dilapidated heap, which had had pretensions of being a castle at one time, would have made with her fair beauty! How very shocked she would have been to see in what manner he had been living. Yes, it was a very good thing that he had had that little chat with Toby. It would never have done. Not at all! He must see to it at once. The very first thing Monday. And he was sure he had no need of Toby's company on that little journey. He could undertake to find himself a housebuilder with help from no one. After all it was his house and his decision.

But what of Lady Katherine? he wondered. It was one thing to say that he had a tendre for her. He was sure that every young man in the district could have put forth the same claim. But he was a viscount, and that ought to stand him in good stead. He was become quite wealthy, too, possibly on a par with Earl Lovelace, her father. Actually, if he thought about it, time was running out on him. The Lovelaces were not in the district forever. It was just that at this time of year they spent a few months in the country on their estate beyond Kirklington. If he was to say anything to Katherine, it had better be said before she returned to London for her second season. It was odds against her having a third season as a maid, for he could not doubt but that she had had many offers.

And that could be a bit of a rub right there. She

was but eighteen and he was in his thirties. How must he appear to her? Deucedly silly question, that. She could barely know him. As he had not partaken of the social activities of the neighborhood to any extent, there was but a nodding acquaintance between them.

Well, he thought, he had better remedy that and right away. If the fair young thing was to evince an interest in him, he had better give her some opportunity to get to know him. And what could be a better time than this very moment? He could ride right out to Kirklington and pay a call.

He spurred his mount and went sailing down the road, only to pull hard on his reins and shout, "Whoa!"

Not only was he not dressed to pay a call upon such a vision of loveliness, he had not a thing at home worthy of her sight. By damn! that was something else he would have to see to. Perhaps he ought to have gone to London. What could he expect to find in a Nottingham tailor's shop worthy of a viscount?

But London was so very far away and it would take all that much more time for a tailor to sew him up a respectable garment. No, he would just have to make do in Nottingham. He would buy the best that was obtainable from the best tailor in the town. Surely, within a week he would be outfitted in clothing such that he need not be ashamed of his appearance in the local society.

He turned his horse off the road and into the fields, riding cross-country back to his estate.

It was Friday afternoon and Mr. Thorpe was feeling quite lonely, cooped up in his small office wondering what his wife and his niece were up to. He was quite willing to admit that the place had not been quite the same since he and Miranda had come to their business arrangement. Things had settled down to a much slower pace than he was used to. There had been no quarrels erupting in the drawing room, no complaints from Crenshaw that his niece would not let him proceed with his work. Even Piper appeared to be subdued—and it had all happened in a day.

He had brought Miranda into the workroom and instructed his two young men to give her something to keep her busy, to assist her only to the extent that she required it, and to get on with their own work. He had expected that there would be trouble with the new apprentice. Miranda had such feminine ideas about architecture, which were always cause for great debate. He had insisted that, if she wished to learn the work and to contribute to it, until she understood all that was involved, she had to do as she was told or not at all. Perhaps that bit of wisdom on his part had turned the trick. Miranda had been given her own space, drawing tools, and paper and had set to work upon a column that would support his grace's roof. It was something that either Piper or Crenshaw could have done in a day, but he was satisfied that it would keep Miranda busy for a month. She had no knowledge of loads and stresses, and she would profit from an opportunity to learn precisely how far from a lady's interest the work of architectural planning and construction was.

It was now the fourth day. Miranda had done her bit of work for two days; today was the second of the alternate days at home with Martha. The office was quiet, too quiet.

The first lady architect, Mr. Thorpe mused. No, things had not come to that yet. But the drawing that Miranda had completed, which was at that moment spread upon the desk before him, was a most commendable piece of work. It was neither better nor worse than an effort by Crenshaw, who was quite competent. Mr. Thorpe was given to wonder just how much Crenshaw had helped her with it—but he had been afraid to inquire. Somehow it made him feel like a beekeeper about to stir up a hive of his nasty little charges.

Miranda was bound to see some sort of compliment in it and there would be the devil to pay with her if she had managed to do the bit all by herself, a possibility he strongly suspected to be true. She was not an unintelligent girl by any means and was quite prone to use her wit to his discomfiture, such as insisting that she be given even greater responsibility than the laying out of a simple column.

He felt uneasy on another score as well. The column was derived from a work of Vitruvius's, and she had not made the smallest objection. That did not speak at all well for what his niece had in mind. Miranda was not a sweet female like dear Martha. No, she was a true Thorpe, every bit as sharp as she could be. He had ever to be on his guard with her if he wished to keep the advantage. Somehow he had the distinct impression that Miranda had gotten the upper hand with him. She had been too quiet, too sweet, and much too obliging for him to believe otherwise.

He sighed. It would be good if he could join his wife and niece this very moment and listen to them chatting. He might get a clue to the validity of his worries about his niece that way.

The thought was very strong in him and he decided he would close the office earlier this day. The work for Roxbury was well in hand. There were some other commissions to be begun, but there was no rush.

Yes, he smiled, things had quite turned around for an architect fortunate enough to have located his business in Nottingham. There was a lot of new-made wealth coming into the city and the shire: The great new machinery that was spitting out hundreds of yards of cloth in a day and requiring monstrous sheds to house them—architect's work. Naturally, the proprietors, making money hand over fist, required abodes to match their new positions of affluence—architect's work, again. And, he grinned to himself, the landed aristocracy refused to be outdone by the new wealth and were having a hard look at their own ancestral homes with an eye to their improvement—more architect's work!

He did not mind in the least that, because his office was so overwhelmed with commissions, architects from Oxford and even London had to be brought in on occasion. No, he did not mind at all. There was more work than a dozen architects could handle, and more coming in all the time. The world was changing, and an architect could make a fortune for himself even if he never achieved the notice of a Sir Christopher Wren. Aye, leave St. Paul's of London to Wren. Perhaps, someday, they will look upon Nottingham and see the work of Thorpe!

For a moment, in his mind's eye, he was actually able to enjoy the sight of that famous city completely reconstructed à la Thorpe and Brother, and, when Mr. Piper put his head in at the door to announce a visitor, he was greatly disturbed to see his version of what Nottingham ought to look like come tumbling down in ruins.

"Yes, what is it?" he demanded impatiently. He took a card from the junior architect's hand and scanned it.

His eyebrows shot up in surprise. It was a nobleman, the owner of a very fine home to the north of the city. He did not number himself among this young gentleman's acquaintances and, therefore, he could not see any reason for the visit.

He shrugged and said, "Show the gentleman in."

As Squire Trimwell came in, Mr. Thorpe rose and gave him a cordial greeting. Offering him a chair, he tried to think what business had brought this noted sporting figure to his office. He had not a clue, so he said, "Sir Tobias, it is an unlooked-for pleasure to have you call upon me. In what way can I serve you, sir?"

Sir Toby replied, "I am told, sir, that you build houses." He looked about him and went on. "If you do, it sinks me how you do it. I should think you would need a gang of chaps, something mightier than the two specimens I passed on my way in to you. If you will pardon my saying so, sir, you do not look the sort who'd be at home with a saw or a hammer in his hands."

Mr. Thorpe laughed with delight. "Ah, yes, you have got a tremendous sense of humor, Sir Tobias. You know very well that this is an office of architects, and very little construction work goes on within its walls, heh, heh! But perhaps it is not with regard to a commission that you have come?"

Sir Toby frowned, for he was a little lost. "Quite so," he said. "As a matter of fact, I have come only to determine if you chaps build homes. I can see that I have come to the wrong place—"

"Oh, no, my dear sir, not at all. Indeed we do accept commissions for the construction of a home, a shop, an inn, a church, what have you."

"I haven't a thing in that regard, sir, but I have got a friend—a neighbor, in fact—who is of a mind to buy himself a house, because the rubble heap he is living in at present must defeat anyone who attempts to do it up properly."

"Ah, then you have come to me as an agent, sir."

"Not at all! I have come to tell you that this friend of mine needs a house. Can you build him one?"

"But of course I can. That is my business, sir, as I have just informed you. Now where—"

Sir Toby shook his head doubtfully. "Are you sure, sir? I imagine that putting a great thing like a house together is a bit more work than you are up to at your age."

Mr. Thorpe blinked and rubbed his chin. "Is it possible, Sir Tobias, that you did not understand me to say that I am a fully qualified architect?"

"But you said you can build a house for my friend. It is a housebuilder he is in need of."

"But before a house can be built it has to be designed, sir. That is what an architect is for—to design the place and then see to it that it is built according to plan."

"So that is how it is, is it? Well then, I have come to the right place after all," declared Sir Toby proudly.

Mr. Thorpe reached for his handkerchief and began to mop his brow. "Quite. Now may I inquire as to the identity of this friend and neighbor of yours?"

"The Viscount Farnsworth of Farnsfield, sir."

"Farnsfield? Do we have a viscount in that neighborhood? I am not acquainted with your district, Squire."

"Lord Farnsworth has not been very active. He has been inclined to see to his estate and has little time for anything else. The thing of it is, he expressed a wish for a better residence, and I took it upon myself to determine how one goes about arranging for such an undertaking."

"I see. May I suggest that Lord Farnsworth let me know in some detail his desires in the matter? I should be only too happy to call upon the gentleman at his convenience—or, if he should prefer it, I will be more than pleased to meet with him in this office."

Sir Toby nodded his head. "And that is all there is to it?"

"For the time being, yes, sir. I shall have to go into various aspects of his lordship's wishes with regard to space and appearance. I shall have to visit the grounds to examine what the site he has selected will allow in the way of construction. But

I am sure his lordship is aware of this sort of thing."

Sir Toby shook his head. "No, I do not think so, or he'd have done something about it right off. Thorpe, I venture to say that you will have to explain it all to him as you have to me. I am sure I understand the business perfectly now, but unfortunately it is not I who am in need of a house. You see, I have a most excellent habitation. It is called Winkwood—you see, it borders on Winkbourn as well as Kirklington, which is actually my seat. If you ride up to Farnsfield, you won't catch a glimpse of it, because Kirklington is to the north of Farnsfield—to the northwest, actually."

"How interesting," murmured Mr. Thorpe, wishing more than ever that he was at home with Martha and Miranda at that moment.

"Yes," said Sir Toby, rising smartly and holding out his hand. As Mr. Thorpe, a little dazed, stood up and shook his hand, Sir Toby declared, "Thorpe, I thank you. Indeed, it is a pleasure to do business with you. Good day, sir."

He turned and briskly marched out of the office, a very self-satisfied look upon his countenance.

CHAPTER IV

If it had not been a Sunday, Lord Farnsworth, out of all patience, would have traveled down to Nottingham and visited a tailor. He felt something of a fool. If he had had the good sense to go to the city on Friday, he could have paid a call upon Lady Katherine today.

Sober reconsideration showed him the fallacy of his thinking. The tailor would still require a few days' time to cut and sew at least one of the garments he planned to order. He could not possibly have had it done before Tuesday, even in London. He would just have to be patient and wait until the next Sunday to begin paying court.

Still, he had no taste for poring over his books of accounts, as he had spent many a Sunday in the past, and he had grown fearfully bored with his lonely existence. The gloomy, decrepit rooms in which he ate and slept added nothing to his ease now that he knew he could afford so much better accommodations.

He decided that enough was enough; he would ride up to Kirklington and call upon Sir Toby. There was always something doing in that quarter, and he wished for diversion. Toby might be very surprised to see him, but he had no doubt that Toby would be pleased as well.

There were two ways to ride over to Kirklington and, with regard to the distance traversed, there was little to choose between them; but the one went by the village of Edingley, which had nothing to attract a traveler whereas the other went past Upper Hexgreave. Set within Hexgreave Park was the residence that housed the Right Honorable the Earl Lovelace, his countess, and his fair daughter, the Lady Katherine. Lord Farnsworth took the more attractive avenue.

He did not think to meet with anyone on his ride to Kirklington; he just had a wish to view where she lived and have a dream or two as he rode past. He was dressed as well as his limited wardrobe could afford, and that was a deal less than the latest fashion. In Sir Toby's company, he did not think his apparel would be at all exceptional.

It was not a pretty day. The sky was filled with rolling gray clouds that obliterated the sun and warned of a change to come. Fitful breezes stirred up dust along the road, and the ride was not as pleasant as it might have been.

He came up to the crossroads and turned off to the left towards Kirklington, proceeding at a walk. Twenty minutes of slow riding brought him around the bend where the western boundary of Hexgreave Park came to the road. He sat up in his saddle and looked out towards the great house of the Lovelace family, studying it from.all the angles that presented themselves to him as he traveled along.

In a little while he was deep in a study of the sort of house he ought to have built for himself. Hexgreave Hall was very large and gave a blockish appearance, even though the two towers that sprouted from alongside the main portal surmounted the roof line. Lord Farnsworth did not consider himself a critic of architecture but thought that a house such as Hexgreave Hall would suit him admirably, especially as it would be the sort of place that Lady Katherine was quite used to. If ever a man had good reason for selecting a particular fashion of edifice for his home, that it resembled his lady's original home seemed a good one. So Lord Farnsworth believed, and the idea so appealed to him that he made a special note of the hall so that he could instruct his housebuilder, when he had found him, how he was to proceed.

There was a further beauty to the idea, he found. A house that was square could easily be fitted with rooms. He could imagine a grid of chambers laid out to fill a box of a house. Of course one had to add a corridor here and there so that access to the various parts was easy. Then, too, space would have to be reserved for staircases so that one could get up and down. Then, of course, there was the question of doors to the outside.

That last thought gave him pause. One did not like to have a door opening out of every room and that must call for but a few doors with corridors running all about so that the inhabitant of any room could manage to find his way out of the building in a reasonably convenient manner. On further consideration, the business seemed to take on a complexity that bore no relation to the simple shape of the house. His lordship came to believe that he might require assistance just to plan the structure. Nevertheless, in addition to knowing the lady that he wanted for his wife, he now was assured that he understood quite well the style of abode he would require. He urged his horse along the road at a slightly faster pace, wishing to impart to his friend Toby the wonderful conclusion he had arrived at.

He turned in his saddle for a last view of Hexgreave Hall, regretting that he was not dressed suitably to make a call there, and then turned his thoughts to his arrival at Winkwood. Sir Toby's estate was two miles beyond Kirklington, and he had to ride through that village on his way.

He came round the sharp bend just beyond the village and espied two riders dallying by the wayside. He recognized Sir Toby and, to his astonishment, Lady Katherine. Color mounted to his cheeks as the young squire looked up from his conversation with her ladyship and greeted him. He felt very put out that Lady Katherine should see him at such a disadvantage, but as she was smiling cordially in his direction, he put a good face on it and drew up alongside them.

He was a little nervous as he exchanged comments on the day's weather but was devastated when Lady Katherine remarked, "Sir Toby has informed me that the neighborhood is about to be blessed with a great new house, my lord. How very exciting!"

Lord Farnsworth was not happy. This was not the way he had hoped the knowledge of his plan would come to her ladyship's ears. His glance at Sir Toby was filled with annoyance as he replied, "Indeed, Lady Katherine, it is my intention to remove myself from the present house to an abode more fitting to my circumstances."

Giving him a pert glance over her shoulder, she asked, "And pray tell, who is the mysterious stranger you have selected to be your viscountess?"

Her smile as she asked was so utterly charming, Lord Farnsworth felt thankful to be mounted, for the sudden weakening in his knees would otherwise have imperiled his aplomb.

It was too much for his lordship. He wheeled

upon Sir Toby and exclaimed, "Really, Toby, have you no respect for a confidence?"

Sir Toby's jaw dropped. "I say, old chap, you never put it that way! Besides you never revealed the lady's name. Blast! A chap's bound to wed sooner or later, and there is, invariably, a lady in the case. Seems to me, Tony, you said nothing exceptional to me and I said nothing exceptional to Lady Katherine here as a result."

"The thing of it is that nothing is set. I mean to say, how will it look now if I do not rush out at once to the church? I am not ready, for the simple reason that I have got to get a house built, you see," he argued.

Toby shook his head. "No, no, no one is going to think anything about it, I assure you. Why, there are folk who have been engaged to wed for years, never took the step, and passed away before they could. I am sure no one had a word to say about it. Is not that so, Kate?"

It gave Lord Farnsworth a turn to hear Sir Toby address Lady Katherine so informally, but he quickly forgot his jealousy when she replied, "Oh, but surely, Lord Farnsworth, you are not planning to build a new house as a surprise for your bride. She will be surprised, I grant you, but I am inclined to believe that she would regret—and, I would add, rather strongly—that she had not been consulted in the selection of the style of architecture and the arrangement of the chambers within."

Lord Farnsworth, feeling that he was on firm ground, smiled superiorly and declared, "Ah, but I have taken care of that. The house I plan to build will be as much like the one in which she resides at present as two peas in a pod. In short, I plan to build a twin to her father's house."

Sir Toby's eyes lit up with approval. He was about to make an agreeable comment when he happened to glance at Lady Katherine and noted that she was frowning crossly. His smile disappeared in an instant as he too frowned and shook his head knowingly.

Lady Katherine asked testily, "I pray, my lord, that you will be kind enough to inform me what her father's house has to do with anything? My father's house, as everyone knows, is in the poorest taste; if it did not go back generations as the family seat, it would have been pulled down ages ago. I should think that any reasonable female would give anything for the chance to plan her own domicile and not have to put up with accommodations, barely worthy of the name, that some ancient fiddle-faddler from a benighted age wrought, completely unmindful of the demands of a modern household. I know I should deem such an opportunity a blessing!"

Lord Farnsworth could immediately see the excellent sense her ladyship was making and waxed enthusiastic.

"Would you really?!" he exclaimed almost gleefully.

"Of course she would. She just said she would. Wouldn't you, Kate?" Sir Toby rejoined.

"But of course. I know she did. I—" said Lord Farnsworth.

"And what is needed is an architect," announced Sir Toby, sagely.

Lady Katherine regarded him with slight disdain. "Toby, I am sure any fool knows that."

Both gentlemen immediately agreed wholeheartedly with her.

At that point, Lady Katherine slipped out a little watch from a pocket in her habit and remarked, "If you gentlemen will be so kind, I am expected at home—"

Lord Farnsworth and Sir Toby were immediately at her service to see her home. The little party turned and headed back toward Hexgreave Hall.

Lord Farnsworth stayed Sir Toby as they came out onto the highroad after having taken leave of Lady Katherine on her doorstep.

"Toby, I would have a bit of conversation with you."

"Quite, old chap. Bit of a smasher, ain't she?" he said with a chuckle.

47

"I say, how did you know I wished to speak of her ladyship?"

"I didn't. Thought you wished to discuss the house. Found an architect fellow for you, you know. Looked a bit old in the tooth to be a house-builder, but you heard her ladyship. Any fool knows one has to have an architect. I say, are all architects ancient chaps? This one is—ah, but I told you that already. Care for a younger chap myself, but there you are. He is right down there in Nottingham. Says he'll wait upon your pleasure. Has a couple of drawing chaps with him, but I saw never a tool. Now, I ask you, how the devil can an old chap like that, with but two pencil-pushers, build you a house? But you heard her ladyship, and I dare say she knows all about the business. Of course I do, too. Found you a blamed architect, didn't I?"

"What! Have you been all over the shire airing my business?" demanded Lord Farnsworth. "Of course I shall have need of an architect. I'd have come to it before long, but I have not had a chance to think the business out. Damme, I have never had occasion to build a house before."

"Yes, and you heard her ladyship on that score, too. Better have your heart's delight do the business for you. How a female comes to housebuilding, I do not know. Home's a man's castle. Never heard it was a female's. But there you are—marry 'em and your house ain't your own!"

Lord Farnsworth made a feeble attempt to stem the torrent but Sir Toby had not finished.

"Now Kate is a different proposition altogether, wouldn't you say? For a female, she knows all about this architect business, and she's a oner for looks into the bargain. Ah well, it is no worry of mine, this business of building a house. Winkwood was put together by an apprentice of Wren's, I've been told, and it has been standing for only a little over a century. Impressive place, if I do say so myself. I say, you've never been to visit. What say we repair to Winkwood and sample some of my stock? I've got some superb Tokay. Cost me eighty-four pounds the dozen. Worth every penny of it, too."

"Thank you. I should be most happy to come and see the place, and perhaps we can talk."

Sir Toby burst into laughter as they both urged their horses into a walk. "Jolly good that. Perhaps we can talk—as if that is not what we have been doing."

The Tokay proved excellent, and Sir Toby's salon, whose windows opened onto a broad lawn in the rear of the house, proved a pleasant place to sit, but Lord Farnsworth was not all that impressed with the building itself. Winkwood was in an excellent state of preservation and its furnishings were spotless—which, of course, attested to a large domestic staff. Farnsfield House could boast only a few cottager's wives who came in to tidy up what few furnishings the late viscount had not seen fit to sell. Seeing the result of a well-run establishment put his lordship in mind of the fact that a new house would require an ample staff of servants, and he had not got even a valet for himself. Needless to say, he experienced some envy as he looked about him at Toby's abode.

Despite the freshness of the place, he did not find himself very much at ease in it and preferred his own dwelling with all its disrepair. He hoped that somehow, when his new house was completed, it would be as comfortable as his old one and still pleasing to Lady Katherine—but, of course, as she would have a hand in its planning, she was bound to be pleased with it.

Putting such matters aside for the moment, he complimented Sir Toby on the Tokay and proceeded with the topic that was uppermost on his mind.

"I note that you address her ladyship as Kate," he remarked.

Sir Toby looked at him in surprise. "I say, Tony, your ignorance is a constant source of amazement to me. The lady's given name is Katherine. Now Kate is short for Katherine, you see. It is really quite simple."

"Ye gods, Toby, you can feel free to credit me with that much wit! The thing is that to call a lady by the diminutive of her name is to imply that you are on informal terms with her and are, in fact, quite friendly with her."

"Right, old chap," and Sir Toby stood and lifted his glass. "My Lady Kate, may her beauty continue to flower!"

Since Lord Farnsworth heartily concurred in the toast, he raised his glass to Sir Toby's and they both drank.

They resumed their seats and Lord Farnsworth demanded, "How do you come to know her ladyship so well?"

"Didn't you know? We have known each other from our earliest days. When I am ready for it, I shall pop the question and we shall be spliced. Why do you frown?"

"You are pledged?"

Sir Toby shrugged. "It hardly matters between childhood sweethearts."

"Blast you! Answer the question: Are you or are you not pledged to Lady Katherine?"

Sir Toby raised his glass and peered into its amber depths. He shook his head as though the answer he was seeking was not to be found in his tumbler. "I say, old thing, what's got you so hot? Can't be the drink, I assure you. Nothing like Tokay, you know."

"Toby, it is not the drink. I asked you a simple question. Can you not give me a simple answer?"

51

"No!"

"You refuse?" asked Lord Farnsworth, shocked.

"Damn it all! You asked for a simple answer and I gave it you! No!"

"Oh!" exclaimed his lordship, falling back in his chair very much relieved.

"Now Tony, old man, because I hold you in friendship I shall disregard the impertinence of your inquiry, but I should like to know—I should bloody damned well like to know: What business is it of yours?"

Lord Farnsworth suddenly felt trapped. True, it had been an impertinent demand he had made of Sir Toby and, because Sir Toby had responded and made a similar demand upon him, he could not refuse to comply. It would have been an out-and-out rebuff.

His face reddened as he said, "Truly, Toby, so long as Lady Katherine has not plighted her troth with you, there is naught to be said against another chap paying court to her with the intention of matrimony, is there?"

Sir Toby frowned. He thought for a moment and then shook his head. "No, I quite agree—not that it will do the beggar the least bit of good, though. He'd have his work cut out for him to put me aside in my lady's regard."

Lord Farnsworth breathed more easily. "Yes, I am quite sure of it. It was just that I was curious, is all."

With a wise look Sir Toby said, "Curiosity is it? You would not be nursing a tendre for her ladyship yourself, would you? But, dammitall Tony, you have no acquaintance with Lady Katherine!"

"That is about to be remedied. You have no objection?"

Sir Toby shrugged. "Not in the least, old man. I'll sit back for a bit and watch the fun, if you do not mind. As I said, I am not quite ready to pop the question, and I do not see that you have any chance with her. I mean no offense, friend, but you are come into the business late and do not strike me as being all that forward. I mean to say, you sit on your hams for five years and now, suddenly, you are out to capture the affection of our beauty." He grinned. "I'll not wish you luck, but I would not be averse to a friendly wager on the outcome."

"I am pleased to see that you take it in good spirit, but this is a most serious business to me. I cannot possibly see it as a bit of sport."

"As you wish, my lord."

At that point, Sir Toby's butler came in with another bottle.

Lord Farnsworth stood up. "That was excellent Tokay, and I thank you for this little chat. I must be going now. I have a great deal to do. By the way, can you suggest a good tailor in Nottingham, old man?"

Sir Toby immediately tried to argue Lord Farnsworth out of patronizing the tailors of Nottingham. They were far behind London when it came to fashion, and any gentleman who was a gentleman must have his apparel from Weston, although he had word that the new chap, Stultz, in Clifford Street, was making a name for himself and might be worth a call.

But time was of the essence for his lordship, and he insisted on the name of a Nottingham establishment. Begrudgingly, Sir Toby gave him a name and directions, but with the admonition that he would never be satisfied, the best of 'em were not on a par with a good London apprentice.

CHAPTER V

Miranda was busily at work in the large anteroom that served as the workroom for the junior architects. Crenshaw and Piper were closeted with Mr. Thorpe, going over a problem that had developed with the plans for the Duke of Roxbury, so that she was quite alone for the moment.

The few days that she had been busy at the desk had been very interesting to her and the bit of studying and drawing she had done had convinced her more than ever that residences could be designed to be homes rather than palaces in miniature. She was resolved that, given the chance, it was how she would plan any such undertaking to which she could win assignment. Knowing her uncle's hidebound devotion to the old masters of architecture, she gave him no hint of her thinking—although, having had her say to him on this point many times before she had been allowed to actually do the work, she was sure that she would have to go softly with him for a while.

The outer office door opened and in walked a tall gentleman of sober mien, his clothes neat but of an unstylish cut. She thought him a gentleman despite his dress because he came to a stand just within the door and stared about him with a dignity that went with rank. She was sure that such fine features as he possessed could only indicate gentle blood.

His gaze came to rest upon her and he frowned.

She arose and made a little curtsy. "Worthy sir, can we be of any assistance to you?"

"These are the offices of Thorpe and Brother, a firm of architects?" he asked.

"Indeed, sir."

"Er—you are obviously neither Mr. Thorpe nor his brother, and it is one or the other I wish to confer with."

"There is only one Mr. Thorpe. His brother, my father, is deceased, sir. At the moment, Mr. Thorpe is engaged with his associates, but I am sure that I can be of assistance. Pray, whom am I speaking with?"

"Ah yes," he said and reached into his pocket for his card case. He fumbled a bit as though it was not a gesture he made often. A little line appeared on Miranda's brow. Finally he succeeded in extricating the case and fingered it to produce a card. Nothing came out, for the simple reason that it was empty. "Oh, I say!" he exclaimed, flushing with embarrassment. "Blast, I do need a man!"

Miranda looked surprised and exclaimed, "A man?"

"I beg your pardon. It is just that if I had

thought to engage a valet, something like this would never have happened. I shall do it the first thing—but, in the meantime, I am Anthony Viscount Farnsworth and I have my seat at Farnsfield. That is what I wish to discuss with your uncle. If he is busy, I am sure I can return when he is not engaged—"

"Oh no, your lordship. Please be seated. I am sure that I can undertake to begin a discussion with you and then you will have saved that much time, you see."

"Miss Thorpe, is it? Miss Thorpe, I did not come to this office to pass the time of day in idle social chatter but to discuss business with an architect. As, obviously, you are not an architect, it stands to reason that my business is with your uncle and not with you," he said with a note of asperity.

"As it happens, Viscount Farnsworth, I am an architect—or will be one before long—and I am certainly sufficiently qualified to conduct a discussion of the initial details of a commission with a degree of intelligence," she replied coolly.

"You are employed here—in this office?" he asked, his eyebrows raised in shock.

"It is what I have been saying, your lordship."

"I think I should prefer a professional gentleman who is not so hard-pressed as to have to engage his female relations in a commerce in which they have no proper place." He turned to leave.

"A moment, your lordship, I pray!" said Miranda forcefully, taking a few paces towards him. "It is not fair of you to judge my uncle's expertise and success by my presence on these premises. I am here not because he is hard-pressed but because I pressed him hard to permit it. I am intensely interested in the design and construction of houses and am employed here only by my own choice and for my own amusement. But that is not to say that I am not serious in the pursuit of this vocation—"

"But you are a female. I never heard—"

"My lord, what has that to say to anything? The fact is that it is women who spend the greatest time in the houses that men build for them. Does it not appeal to your sense of what is proper that a female should have a say in how a home is to be laid out before it is built, instead of having to put up with what some architect—more likely a bachelor with no experience of a modern home and its requirements—dredges up from the depths of a mind filled to overflowing with temples and churches and great monuments? Women do not wish to live in monuments, I do assure you."

"I say!" Lord Farnsworth remained standing with his hand upon the doorknob. "It is strange that you should make that point, Miss Thorpe. It was just the other day I was engaged in a similar discussion, from which I came away impressed with a view quite similar to the one you are espousing." His hand dropped from the doorknob and he took a step into the chamber. "I do believe I should very much like to chat with you about this house that I intend building."

"Oh, I am so pleased, my lord," exclaimed Miranda gleefully. "Please do be seated. Give me but a moment and we can have some tea. You would like some tea, would you not? We can discuss the business of a new house for you at our leisure."

It did not strike the viscount as a particularly businesslike way to proceed but it was certainly a more pleasant way than he could have expected.

When the conference in the inner office came to an end and the two men came back into the workroom to continue with their work, they discovered Miranda sitting on her stool by the window, staring out at the traffic in Upper Parliament Street.

She turned away from the window and inquired, "Have you done with my uncle, gentlemen?"

Upon being informed that indeed they were and that he was as surly as a lion with a thorn in its paw, Miranda snatched up some papers from her table and bustled into Mr. Thorpe's office.

He was intently studying some plans, using a pair of dividers to make comparative measurements. He looked up with a growl. "Go 'way, Miranda. Can you not see that I am occupied?"

"This will not take but a moment, Uncle Sylvester, and it is quite important, I assure you."

He tossed the dividers down with a sigh of exasperation. "What is it, my dear? I swear, since you have come to work here, I am amazed at the sudden influx of mattters of the greatest moment. I am sure I shall never know peace if I were to defer this business of yours for five minutes. Tomorrow is the day your aunt has to put up with you, is it not? But of course it is. How lovely! We might even be able to get a piece of work done in this office."

"My dear, beloved Uncle, I pray you will withhold your pleasantries until you have heard what I have to report. Tomorrow I fear that Aunt Martha will have to suffer through the day without my bright presence, for I am engaged to go up to Farnsfield to pay a call upon the Viscount Farnsworth."

"What is this nonsense?" he demanded impatiently. Then, "Farnsworth? That has a familiar ring to it. Now where have I heard that name before? Why, I do believe there was a chap—a confused beggar if I ever saw one—in about a house for a friend. Knew absolutely nothing of what he was trying to say. Neither did I. So he has come back, has he? Where is he? Why in heaven's name would you wish to pay a call upon that nitwit, may I ask?"

Miranda shook her head in impatience. "No, no,

you have got it all wrong. You must be thinking of someone else. The viscount has not been to see us before this. He has got a house to build and he wishes to have my view before we sit down to plan it. Naturally, I had to tell him that I should have to see the site, and he quite graciously consented to receive me tomorrow."

"But I tell you, I have seen the chap—a squire, is he not? I am sure he is, for he told me so himself—Oh, but wait. That was not he. I mean to say, he had come to speak for his friend and neighbor. But, Miranda, my child, what can you be thinking of? Of course you may not call upon the gentleman! If he is anything like his neighbor—Trimwell, Sir Tobias Trimwell was the style he gave—I'd not trust you with him for a second, not by yourself. And furthermore, my pet, it was never a part of our bargain that you would do anything beyond the confines of these walls. No, of course you are not—Stab me! A *client*! You talked with a client and never informed me? Miranda, this is the outside of enough! Quickly, where is the gentleman? A viscount, you say, and he wishes to build a house? Quickly, I must speak with him. Certainly, I must make abject apology for allowing him to be subjected to the torments of a female flibbertigibbet who does not know her God-given place!"

"Uncle Sylvester! It so happens that Lord Farnsworth was mightily impressed with my view of architecture, and we had a most interesting chat. He will be back shortly—he has a bit of shopping to do—and wishes to sit with you to discuss the business further. Now, how is that for a flibertigib-bet?"

Mr. Thorpe's handkerchief was out and busily mopping his forehead. "Is that a fact, my dear? Then I must say 'Well done.' Well done, indeed. Now you just leave the business and his lordship in my hands and get back to your work. By the way, what in heaven's name are you busy at? Neither Crenshaw nor Piper have a clue."

"They have not a clue for the simple reason that I was designing the house I wish to live in—and that is not any of their business—"

"I say, Miranda, you are not supposed to be working on your own personal undertakings. It is the firm's time—"

"It is the firm's time only if the firm pays for it."

"But it is the firm's paper and the firm's furniture and the firm's instruments."

"Ah, then it is I who must pay the firm for the space I take up. You may deduct it from my pin money, Uncle."

"And have you go about behind my back complaining of your niggardly uncle? Not by far. Ye gods! How do I manage to get into these nonsensical conversations with you? Must we always be debating?"

"Not at all, Uncle dearest. All you have got to do is to sit down with the viscount and me, and we shall all of us go into the business of his new seat together."

"Miranda, be sensible. Of course, you cannot be involved—"

"And why not?" she demanded belligerently. "It was I he sat down with first and it was my ideas he was taken with. I venture to say it was more than you'd have trusted Crenshaw or Piper to do."

"Yes, and I'd never have trusted you either, my pet," he retorted.

"No doubt, but that fat's in the fire and he wishes to build my house."

"*Your* house? This dream of yours you have been at sketching! Why, you have not got the first idea of how to go about it. For example, from whose work have you derived it?"

"My own work!" she replied, indignantly.

"How very sweet. Your own work, is it? You mean to say that you have not borrowed the least bit from Palladio, not a smidgin from Vitruvius? It is your own work?"

"That is precisely what I mean to say."

"In a matter of what? Three days? You have drawn up a complete house, supporting walls and pillars, roofs and chambers, staircases and portals? All of this you have done?"

"But of course I have not done so much, nor am

I claiming to have done so. In any case, for a first discussion, it is hardly necessary. What I have done is to show his lordship an exterior view of what I propose—and you will admit that it was quite fortunate that I had come that far with it, for his lordship thought it would do very well. Now all that you have got to do is to tell the viscount how it will be erected and how much it will cost. Do you see how much time I have saved you? You will not have to go through a business of submitting sketch after sketch as you did to obtain Roxbury's approval. That much is already done."

In tones of mock-sweetness Uncle Sylvester replied, "Has it ever occurred to you, young lady, that there is a little more to the business of designing a house than merely making a pleasing sketch? One has got to draft it according to the principles of proper construction. What good will it do if this beautiful concoction of yours has no strength to it but must tumble to the ground like a house of cards because the design does not allow for its proper support? Let me see that blasted sketch before you say another word!"

Late that afternoon Lord Farnsworth returned to the offices of Thorpe and Brother to find Mr. Sylvester Thorpe all smiles and most cordial.

The master architect himself conducted his lordship into the inner office, and the two gentlemen were closeted together for more than an hour.

Miranda, fuming, waited for fifteen minutes before, in a fit of temper, she clapped on her cloak and walked out of the office, her nose in the air.

"Ah yes, Mr. Thorpe, I begin to understand," said Lord Farnsworth, as he stepped forth from the office with Mr. Thorpe right behind him. "The young lady's sketch was quite charming but, as you say, a mere picture and not a design. Well, I have never had to build a house before, so I ask your pardon if I seem green to you." He sighed. "I had hoped to see the work started at once, and I must admit to disappointment. I never thought that so much had to be taken into account. Well-a-day, I pray you will be submitting your ideas to me as soon as possible. Please feel free to come out to Farnsfield to look over my estate. I had in mind a site for the new house, but after what you have said, I shall have to leave it up to you to see to it."

"Oh, I do beg your pardon, your lordship, for having given you a false impression. I can select a site if that is what you wish, but I think it would be far better if you were to do so, and then I can tell you how we shall build upon it when I have examined it. I mean to say that you are not about to site your house in a marsh or upon the verge of a cliff, if you understand what I mean. It is just that certain types of sites call for certain sorts of construction, and this may or may not, as the case may be, impose limitations upon the final result."

65

Lord Farnsworth was now satisfied that he understood, and he informed Mr. Thorpe that he would be looking forward to his visit. He then took his leave and started for the door; but, before he got to it, he turned and said, "That niece of yours, Miss Miranda. A most intelligent young lady. Is she about? I should like to say a word to her."

At once Mr. Thorpe turned to look about the chamber and demanded of his draftsmen the whereabouts of Miss Thorpe. Upon learning that she had stormed out of the office, he swallowed hard and turned to Lord Farnsworth, making some sort of apology.

His lordship did not feel particularly concerned. Over his shoulder he suggested that Mr. Thorpe bring Miss Miranda out with him. Some of her ideas were worth going over again.

CHAPTER VI

"Oh? So some of my ideas are worth going over again, are they?" said Miranda. "I think not. The Right Honorable Viscount can do without them!" she stormed at the dinner table.

"Now, dear, you are getting upset over nothing at all." Mrs. Thorpe reached over to her niece's hand. "You are not paying attention to your food, my dear, and I know you like it. Fresh Dover sole brought into Nottingham at great expense. Now do take a morsel of it. This viscount can mean nothing to you. Let your uncle worry about the gentleman. I am sure that you have no wish to go to Farnsfield. It is such a little place that I am sure there is not a decent shop within miles of it."

"But, Martha, my love, I need Miranda. His lordship suggested that she accompany me and I dare not refuse," Mr. Thorpe pointed out.

"But I do dare to refuse," retorted Miranda. "He distinctly said that he loved my ideas for a house and then he changed his mind, the fickle monster!"

"Tut, tut, Miranda. That is no proper way to refer to a nobleman. If he is fickle, all well and good, but I do declare he cannot be a monster," chided Mrs. Thorpe.

"Well, he is!"

"Miranda, I pray you will consider that his lordship did ask after you. He has not rejected all your proposals. It is just that I, as a qualified architect, had to take your designs under advisement, you see. I mean to say, they are not in any degree fashionable. Why, there is no portico, there are no columns, no balconies. It is—it is so un-Palladian."

"It is also un-Vitruvian, Uncle, and it was meant to be so. What need is there for columns that support nothing? Why mar the face of the house with balconies that are never used? I would have one or two in the rear, but I was only dealing with the front elevation—"

"Miranda, your sole is getting quite cold. It will have to be sent back to the kitchen for warming," Mrs. Thorpe interrupted.

"Bother the sole!"

"Miranda, that is no way to talk to your aunt—" began Mr. Thorpe, but Miranda was ahead of him.

"Oh, Aunt Martha, I am so sorry," she said. "I did not mean a word of it, but this awful viscount has got me so up in the boughs I do not know what I am saying."

"Now that will be quite enough, Sylvester," Mrs. Thorpe sharply chided her husband. "See what you and this monstrous marquis are doing to the poor child? Why do you not take her with you? You know how much she likes that sort of thing."

"Er—my dear, I do believe that you have not quite got the hang of the conversation. You see, I—"

"Oh, all right, all right," cried Miranda. "If it will make for peace, I shall go with you, Uncle Sylvester. But you may rest assured I do.it only because it is upsetting Aunt Martha so."

Mr. Thorpe was caught with his mouth open. He stared blankly at his niece and slowly but absently lifted up a piece of sole on his fork to his lips. Still quite unaware of what he was doing, he began to chew his mouthful and then he swallowed it. By that time he had regained possession of his wits.

He smiled at his wife and nodded. "Thank you, my dear. Yes, you are quite right. Thank you indeed."

That night back on his Farnsfield estate, for the first time that he had begun to think about the matter, his lordship enjoyed a sense of confidence in the course he had decided upon. Mr. Sylvester Thorpe had assured him that the business of building houses was an old story with him and that he could practically guarantee his lordship's satisfaction with any construction that Thorpe and

Brother conceived, designed, and had erected. He had been inundated by sketches and plans of houses with a commentary that was so far beyond his comprehension that he could not help but be impressed with Mr. Thorpe's depth of knowledge. Nothing conclusive had come of their talk because, as Mr. Thorpe had explained, estimates of materials and labor had to be derived from a thorough understanding of what was wanted, based upon some preliminary drafting. Then, when his lordship could see how the work was to take shape and had approved it, Mr. Thorpe would sit down with his assistants and reckon how much time it would take and how much the undertaking would cost.

Lord Farnsworth thought that this was something more concrete than anything he had ever heard before, and therefore was more than willing to place all his reliance in the master architect. Obviously, his niece Miranda, even as Mr. Thorpe had implied, was not all that familiar with the details of the procedure, and therefore her suggestions must be taken with a grain of salt. Not, Mr. Thorpe had continued to say, that Miss Miranda was so far out in her ideas. It was just that she required a bit of seasoning in the profession which—Mr. Thorpe had winked—he was sure she never would receive. He had the highest hopes that she would be satisfied to settle down with the gentleman of her choice—if she would but choose—and forget this most unfeminine interest of hers.

It had been the inspiration of the moment for him to have suggested that the niece come out with the uncle. He had been impressed with her knowledge—that is, he had been impressed by her before he had sat down with the uncle, the true expert. Nevertheless, she had a certain enthusiasm which he found quite charming, and he thought that she would do marvelously well to provide him with a feminine viewpoint of the construction. He would much rather have had this viewpoint from Lady Katherine—but he could hardly ask her ladyship. He but barely knew her, and it would have been the height of impudence, considering the manner in which he was thinking of her.

On the following day he sent a letter, actually a summons, to his agent in London to come at once, bringing with him a complete statement of his accounts. His discussion with Mr. Thorpe had brought up the subject of money and he wished to know precisely how grand a house he could afford, without extending himself financially. The fortunes of the estate had been turned around to such good purpose that he was sure it would not be necessary.

It was almost noon when a post chaise came rolling up the drive to the front door with Mr. Thorpe and his niece. Lord Farnsworth found himself quite embarrassed to have to go out to

71

greet them. He had no retainers to make them welcome and bring them to him. He made a mental note to engage a butler and a footman along with the valet. Then, as he helped Miss Miranda down from the carriage, he immediately added any number of maidservants to the list in his mind. They would be the very first consideration he would assign to the new butler when he got him. He was sure that a butler would know how to engage females. He was just as sure that he himself did not.

Mr. Thorpe excused himself almost at once and began to walk about the estate, carefully examining the buildings and making copious notes and sketches of the various aspects of the landscape.

Miranda strolled about with his lordship, which pleased him, for he had no wish to chase after Mr. Thorpe.

"I was very much impressed with your uncle's expertise, Miss Miranda, and have every confidence that he will build me a fine residence."

"My lord, I was distressed to learn that you had not liked the sketch I showed you," she responded. "I realize that it was not yet a complete set of plans, but I thought that it—"

"Oh, but I say, Miss Miranda, I found your little sketch quite enchanting. It was only when Mr. Thorpe assured me that houses just are not built in that way that, of course, I yielded to his way of proceeding. I do sincerely hope that you understand—"

"But, my lord, the house I am planning can easily be made over from your present abode. Oh, there might have to be a change or two, but just look about you. The best place for the new house is precisely where your present house is situated. It stands to reason that if you desire a completely new construction, your present abode would have to be razed before the new one could be begun. I know my uncle, and he will give you such staunch pillars and massive fronts, it will be more of a fortress than a fine house. Now, if we were to dismantle the present building down to the ground floor and reface the outer wall with gray brick instead of that ancient, horrid brown sandstone, we would have the beginnings of a very proper mansion for a viscount, my lord."

"Ah yes, I see what you mean. That old stone facing is quite rude. I dare say it was laid on when the house was first erected. Now that would have been in the year 1268. It has worn rather well, wouldn't you say?"

"Indeed, my lord, but the times have changed and the science of architecture has made many advances since that day. It is over time that you had a new abode for your seat. Now then, I envision carrying the construction up an additional three stories—or, if that should prove to be too

73

many chambers, we need only raise it two stories and give you a parapet or curtain wall to top it off. In that way you will have the height without the added expense of an extra story."

"Sort of a false story, in effect," said the viscount.

"Exactly, my lord."

"Rather like cheating, isn't it?" he said unhappily.

"It is not a game, my lord. We are only trying to confer an air of majesty upon the edifice."

"I see. As it will be a rather small family in number to begin with, I should prefer to stop at the second story. I should imagine it might take a generation or two to fill up a place of that size. Yes, I should prefer not to overdo at this stage."

"I quite agree. It would be ever so much cozier a story less. Then I would suggest that we stop at that point and add a tower—no, I have a better idea. If we were to add an entrance porch we would then have a balcony right over the front portal for each level. It would be something like an open tower climbing the front of the building and adding a frame and cover for the drive. Your guests could then dismount in the nastiest weather, well-sheltered."

"Indeed, it sounds interesting. I think I should like to see a sketch of it."

"Or we can go about it in an entirely different manner," she continued. "I should like to see

74

something with a bit more grace, wouldn't you? Now, if you will recall, my lord—oh dear me, I ought to have brought my sketch along with me. In any case, my lord, what I should like to see—"

"I beg your pardon, Miss Miranda, but the projected structure will be mine and it is a matter of what *I* should care to see, I do believe," he said with some asperity.

Miranda blushed and stammered in her confusion. "M-my lord, I d-do humbly beg your pardon. But of course, the matter is entirely up to you. I never meant to say—that is, I was only trying to suggest—"

"Yes, yes, of course, my dear Miss Miranda. I do understand. It is just that I am wondering what your uncle is at that should take him so long."

Even as he uttered the words, Mr. Thorpe made his appearance, coming round the house as he jotted down some last notes on his pad.

"Ah, there you are, your lordship," he said. "I am pleased to say that I have examined your property and recorded all the pertinent information. I shall now return to Nottingham and you will hear from me in a few days."

"I say, Thorpe, what am I to hear? You are going ahead with the house, are you not?"

Mr. Thorpe laughed politely and said, "Lord Farnsworth, never think that I am not. But when one is about to undertake an enterprise that is not only dear to one's heart as one's dwelling must

75

ever be, but dear to one's purse as well, then it behooves me not to rush into the business. Your lordship, the planning and construction of a home is the most sacred duty of an architect. If I may be pardoned for the metaphor, it is very much like the doctor and the—er—body of his patient—"

"That was a simile and not a metaphor," murmured Miranda, but neither gentleman was listening.

"A sacred trust, your Lordship, and one I have had extensive experience in managing."

"Hmmm, yes. Now then, regarding the site, Miss Miranda believes that the present house is admirably sited and so do I. Do you propose to raze it completely?"

"Oh, but your lordship, it is much too soon for me to say. First, I must consult my notes to refresh my memory of the situation, and then I shall have to study how the light will be striking it. I shall have to make a determination of the prevailing winds so that hearths and chimneys may be properly oriented, and then there is the lay of the land and how it permits access to the edifice, so that the approaches can be properly drawn. What I mean to say is that these are but a few of the considerations that have to be taken into account before a line can be drawn—"

"Then I am to understand it will be some few days before you can decide upon the site of the building."

"Indeed, your lordship—but that is not to say that my decision is in any way final. It must meet with your approval, of course."

"If that is so, I am inclined to prefer that we do not totally raze the present structure and that we begin with the ground floor, replacing the facing with gray brick—"

"Oh, but your lordship, you go too fast. You go too fast indeed! One must approach these situations with a deal of care."

"Yes, I understand that, Thorpe, but Miranda and I were chatting, and she thought—"

"I beg your pardon, Lord Farnsworth, but I must offer my apologies for my niece. Indeed, I am so very pleased that you and Miss Miranda had a pleasant conversation, but—"

"Uncle Sylvester, a word with you please!" demanded Miranda, her eyes snapping. "By your leave, my lord." She snatched her uncle's arm and dragged him off. When she was satisfied they were out of earshot of the viscount, she said in a harsh whisper, "Uncle Sylvester, you are ruining everything!"

Mr. Thorpe's face was flushed with anger. "And you, niece, are trying to drown me in as pretty a kettle of fish as I have ever heard of! Who are you to tell a client, much less me, your uncle, how to manage my affairs? Do you think this is the first time that I have undertaken to build a house for a gentleman? Have you gone over the property, examining the soil and the vistas? Have you done a thing but make a drawing which any young lady who has had your advantages could do? Have you done a thing but spend an hour with his lordship in idle conversation—"

"There was nothing idle about it! The gentleman is in a rush for a house, and I have conceived of one for him which he likes. It is utter foolishness to go on like this, since you know as well as I do that there is not the least necessity for razing his house below the ground floor. There will be quite enough to do fashioning a commodious first floor and a second as well—"

"You know that and I know that, but that is not to say that his lordship knows it. Look you, Miranda, I will thank you to let me handle this business, *my business,* in *my* fashion. Now I pray you will be silent during the remainder of this discussion or I shall forbid you the freedom of my offices, do you understand me? I am the architect and I shall say what his lordship requires! Is that understood?"

"But, Uncle—"

"Not another word! You are succeeding in making a fool of me before the viscount!"

"Very well, but I shall insist upon seeing what you are going to suggest to Lord Farnsworth when you have got it done."

"Very well. We can debate the matter at that

78

time—not this. Come now, we must return to his lordship. I could wish you would say something to put him at his ease so that we may continue in the usual manner."

Miranda nodded and they strolled back to Lord Farnsworth, who looked worried.

"My lord," said Miranda, smiling brightly. "I fear that there was a slight misunderstanding. What I had been suggesting was, or course, mere thoughts which my uncle will certainly take into account as they might fit the actual case. I pray you will be assured that your wishes in the matter will be consulted and your suggestions, as far as they can be made to march with the principles of architecture and good construction, will be followed."

At that point Mr. Thorpe stepped in. "Your lordship, I should like to add that my niece has an intense interest in the subject but, like any female, when it comes to matters of technical expertise, she is not quite at home with the subject. That is why, you may be sure, the mastery of architecture has been reserved to the judgment of men. Now then—"

"Oh, but I say, Thorpe, that has nothing to say to the fact that a lady knows what she likes and what she does not like in a house. I was interested to hear what your niece had to suggest for the very reason that the house I build will one day serve as the residence for a viscountess, my wife, and I should hope that she would be quite happy in it. As a matter of fact, I had better warn you right off, whatever plans you do submit to me will be scrutinized by a lady—er, now you must hold this matter in the strictest confidence—but I have the intention of marrying, and that is why I must have a fine house." Lord Farnsworth was looking quite troubled. There was uncertainty in his eyes as he said again, "You will not mention this—for, as a matter of fact, things have not progressed at all in that direction, you understand."

"Good heavens, Lord Farnsworth!" exclaimed Miranda. "Do you mean to say that you have got to build her a house to win the fair lady?"

"No, I do not!" he snapped. "It is merely that I cannot ask a lady's hand when I have not a decent home to take her to should she accept."

Miranda gave a flirt to her head and retorted, "If I loved a man, I would not care what sort of house he had, be it palace or hovel!"

"Miranda! I am sure that that is Lord Farnsworth's business and none of yours!" chided Mr. Thorpe. Quickly he turned to his lordship and said, "Once again your lordship, I must beg your pardon for the excesses of my niece. As you can see, she has a knack of acting the schoolgirl every now and again. One would think that at the age of four-and-twenty she would have learned to behave better—"

"Uncle Sylvester! I am quite sure that the viscount is not interested in a recounting of my faults or anything else. I do believe that we have done what we have come for and need not take up any more of his lordship's time."

As they took their leave, his lordship's face was red with embarrassment, Mr. Thorpe's face was red with anger, and Miranda's face was red with something of both emotions.

CHAPTER VII

That evening, as Lord Farnsworth sat at table to partake of a lonely supper, resentment began to stir within his breast. The business of the house was not going well. It was not going well at all. He had the distinct feeling that everyone had an idea of what the new house ought to be like and, while no two were in agreement, his own views appeared to stand a very small chance of even being listened to.

As he toyed with the food on his plate before him—it was the usual tepid collation that one of the farm women had prepared, as was the custom in his pinched ménage—he was filled with a great dissatisfaction. He wanted a change, but the more he tried to accomplish it, the more hindrances seemed to rise up. If Thorpe were able to move directly on Miss Miranda's suggestions, if Toby had never been a childhood playmate of Lady Katherine, if all these past years he had been able to devote himself to an already flourishing estate instead of having to revive a moribund one, if . . .

He took a mouthful, made a face, and swallowed it without chewing. It was cold and horrid.

He shoved the plate from him and got up from the table.

On the morrow, he was to go down to Nottingham to try on his new clothes for the final fitting. He would wait for the tailor to do them up and then he must seek out domestic help. It was ridiculous his having to put up with such privation now that he had restored to the Farnsworth name its financial luster. Then, at least, he would be able to curb his impatience while the new house came into being.

Miranda was distinctly dissatisfied with the way the morning spent with Lord Farnsworth had progressed. She was sure that she had made a good beginning with him with regard to the house that she had set her heart upon. In fact, she was sure that it was a second beginning because, until Lord Farnsworth spoke with Uncle Sylvester the first time, he had appeared quite pleased with the sketch she had shown him. Then, out at Farnsfield, Uncle Sylvester had stepped in once again to defeat her wishes. Uncle Slyvester had become quite the villain with her, she thought.

It gave her a pang to consider how helpless his lordship had appeared. The poor man did not seem to have the vaguest idea of what he wanted in a house and she was quite certain that her house would suit him right down to the ground.

Truly it was bad of Uncle Sylvester to have intervened, but she was not about to allow him to defeat her. She would have to bide her time, but one way or another, she would convince his lordship of precisely the house he needed. In the meantime, she would apply herself in the office and learn all that she must to insure that when her house was being built it was all being done quite correctly. She would have to bother Crenshaw a bit, but he, for all his grumbling at being interrupted in his work, was never the one to bring their conversations to an end. As for Mr. Piper, she did not think much of him except as he served to make Mr. Crenshaw a little bit jealous when she paid Mr. Piper some little notice.

Sir Toby would never have admitted it to any one, not even himself, but he was uneasy. Ever since his little chat with Farnsworth, life had taken on a pall and he was not at all comfortable with it. It was just not his way.

Nothing could have been more satisfying to a man of Sir Toby's temperament than to consider how fortune had dealt with him. She had blessed him with great strength and agility and then had done it up brown by bringing him forth as a Trimwell, a member of a fine family that had been prosperous for generations in the Shire of Nottingham. Winkwood was a jewel of an estate that seemed to manage itself. At least, the actual care of the farms and the fields had never been of concern to Sir Toby. Family retainers, with wisdom stimulated by comfortable stipends, had looked after things and kept the incomes of Winkwood from shrinking. They were helped not a little by the fact that their master, for his amusement, rarely ever lost a wager.

Yes, Sir Toby loved to gamble but he was no great risk-taker. His wagers were always laid in the field of sport and never at the gaming tables. Since he was a sportsman of no mean prowess, his chances of winning his wagers were excellent: he was invariably betting upon his own performance and knew to a T how he would fare. Be it boxing, riding, driving, or heaving weights—whatever it was—it was bound to be an activity in which Sir Toby excelled.

In the pursuit of this love, Sir Toby was given to much bragging, so that athletic contests were always his for the asking; however, when he suspected that a prospective competitor might prove more than a match for him, his self-praise became muted, so that he was rarely forced to face a superior competitor. In this way his purse was never drained by his wagering and his estate was never put to strain to keep him in pocket money.

Such habits, coupled with such affluence, gave to Sir Toby a sense of superiority, especially over his neighbor the viscount. Farnsworth had been possessed of a far greater holding than Winkwood and yet had been forced to spend all his time in tending it. The fellow was no sportsman at all and his contacts with him had been quite meager. Never in Sir Toby's experience of Lord Farnsworth had he ever considered the nobleman anything but a poor excuse, a chap who had fallen upon hard times and therefore could be condescended to despite his more exalted rank. It added to Sir Toby's sense of self-satisfaction that, with the exception of Earl Lovelace, he was the wealthiest man in the district.

But it seemed that things had changed, and drastically so. Lord Farnsworth had proved himself something of a grind. His unstinting devotion to his estate had more than recouped the family fortunes, or he would not be talking of replacing the ancient family pile with a brand-new, modern edifice. Nor would he be interested in wedlock.

There was the rub! Sir Toby had cause for great pride in his perception. It had come to him only the very next day that Farnsworth had his eye upon Lady Katherine. Until recently Sir Toby would have laughed at the presumption of the viscount. Now, it was a matter to be pondered. If Farnsworth had been any sort of a sporting chap, he would have been, with regard to the hand of Lady Katherine, a man to contend with. Although he was not as strong as Sir Toby, he cut a fine figure and was an inch or two taller. But beyond those small advantages, as Sir Toby saw them, he had a fearsome taste in apparel, never appearing in anything but the roughest sort of country togs, looking forever like some fieldhand fresh from the toil—which was actually the case. The fool was known to get his hands filthy with the muck of his fields—most unworthy of a gentleman and downright disgraceful in a viscount!

Still, things had changed. Farnsworth, who usually had no more than a greeting for him and a word on the weather, was now talking of new houses and of matrimony, and Lady Katherine was just about the only female in the district to attract the eye of a wealthy viscount.

A viscount! Now precisely how would Lady Katherine feel about that? Sir Toby had never before given the point any thought. Lady Katherine, as the daughter of an earl, would make a superb knight's lady, but might she not consider that a trifle beneath her when she could have the title of viscountess? Most disturbing!

In the end, Sir Toby pooh-poohed the whole idea of Lord Farnsworth having the least chance with Lady Katherine—so long as he, Sir Toby, spent the rest of the day making a tour of his house with an eye to what improvements might be called for to please an earl's daughter. The task proved to be beyond him and he resolved to go into Nottingham to consult with the architect, Thorpe—not so much on his own business as to find out how Farnsworth's plans were progressing, and in how grand a direction.

* * *

Lady Katherine was bored. Nottinghamshire was a most undistinguished place in which to reside, and this particular district was exceedingly sparse in the number of gentlemen—worthwhile gentlemen, that is—to afford her diversion: It was nothing like London.

She knew, without being told, that she was quite the prettiest lady in that part of the shire—but that was a poor laurel when, even though she was not the greatest beauty to appear upon the London scene, in the city she was always surrounded by gentlemen of every rank, degree, and attraction. She had easily concluded that it was far better to be one of many belles with admirers enough for all than a great beauty with never enough eligible admirers to count upon the fingers of one hand.

Actually, in the parish of Southwell, which included the Lovelace family seat, there were perhaps a half-dozen gentlemen who might qualify for her notice. There was, of course, good old Toby, always underfoot and not a brain in his head, but still with something about him to turn the head of any female with an appreciation for a man of action. Then there were John Venture, Robert Fallard, and Freddie Holme. She was never quite sure of their pretensions to rank, but none of them would ever inherit more than a baronetcy. Then there was Viscount Farnsworth, a strange sort of person. He might be attractive if he ever learned to dress properly, but she could not remember ever having seen the nobleman dressed within a year of the latest fashion. He might take a lesson from Toby. Nevertheless, he was a viscount.

But Lord Farnsworth never went about. In fact, it was quite amazing that he had come upon Toby and her that day and stayed to have a conversation. But then, he was about to be wed. What sort of female would be sufficiently attracted to him? Oh, he was not bad-looking, and she understood that he was grown quite wealthy in recent years. The earl, her father, was very much impressed with the viscount and talked endlessly about having him over to dinner some evening. Thank heaven he never got round to sending the invitation.

But then, had not Toby warned her to look for great changes in that gentleman's direction? Indeed he had! There was talk of a new house to be erected at Farnsfield for the new viscountess—and Lord Farnsworth was being seen making the rounds of the Nottingham shops. Now that was very interesting, and she began to try to picture what the new Viscountess Farnsworth would be like and what her antecedents might be.

If Farnsfield was to become something of a showplace and if Lord Farnsworth was to become something of a beau, then how might she feel to be invited to the wedding, the most beautiful girl in attendance upon a bride so obviously her inferior in every way?

She was not sure. She was not sure that she might not wish to be the new viscountess. True, she was an earl's daughter and still quite young, but that was no warranty that she would find herself a husband of equal rank with her father. Here was a viscount who, in her father's estimation, might be a catch and, in her own eyes, might have some promise, seeing that he was in the process of making changes. Only her mother, the countess, took exception to Viscount Farnsworth, and that simply because the gentleman was "too high in the instep to come calling upon them." Lord Farnsworth did not seem to be that sort at all. In fact, all things considered, Lady Katherine concluded she ought to evince some particular interest in the gentleman just to see what, if anything, came of it. She would begin by passing by Farnsfield and inquiring as to the progress of the new house.

CHAPTER VIII

"Lord Farnsworth? Lord Farnsworth!" cried a voice from behind his lordship as he came striding out of St. James Street into Market Place. He was attired from head to foot in apparel that was but freshly purchased. His boots, his suit and coat, his tophat, his stick, even his linen had all been put on in the past few hours that he had spent in Richardson's, where all had been assembled for his approval. It had been such a long time since his lordship had allowed himself the pleasure of fine clothes that he saw no good reason for putting it off a moment longer. On the spot, he placed his order, for more of the same, allowing some variations in style, and donned what had been made ready for him. Thinking it was a fine day, Lord Farnsworth then decided to take a stroll about the town just to get himself accustomed to the not too comfortable boots and the restrictions of a high, starched neckband in place of the heavy field footgear and neckerchief he was used to wearing on his estate.

Hearing his name called, he turned and espied Miss Miranda Thorpe waving at him from across the Market Place. He gestured to show her that he recognized her and then, cane knob held up to his lip, he self-consciously sauntered across the square to greet her.

Miranda smiled as she held out her hand to him and said: "Oh, my lord, you look positively stunning. I do not think I have ever seen you in such stylish fashion. Indeed, you make a most handsome figure."

"Oh, indeed! I thank you, Miss Miranda. As a matter of fact, I have just come from the haberdasher's. I thought what a shame it would be not to have a new wardrobe to go with the new house."

"And the new wife, my lord?"

"I say, how did you know?" he asked, startled.

"Why, you mentioned the fact when I came out with my uncle to Farnsfield. I am dying to know what she is like. I do not suppose you would care to tell me now, would you?"

He smiled to see her so curious. "All in good time, Miss Miranda. First things first, you know. Speaking about the house, does your uncle have anything prepared for me as yet? I am in town for the day, and it would be a saving if we could go over whatever it is that he had concluded thus far."

Miranda's brow clouded. "My lord, are you so set against all that I suggested? I mean to say, the sketch that I showed to you and my suggestion for saving the ground floor and the gray brick facing?"

"Oh dear, do we have to go over that again? I had hoped we had got a little farther along. Perhaps as high as the first floor—but good heavens, if we are still on the gray brick then we have not really got started, have we?"

"Oh, Uncle Sylvester is quite prepared to submit a plan for your approval, but it is nothing like what I had wished. You see, he has an aversion to Wren and would hark back to Palladio with a heavy Gothic influence, which is becoming all the rage now. But it is too much, I do assure you, my lord. What I would say, if it were my house, is 'Something simpler, if you please, Mr. Thorpe.' That is exactly what I would say to my uncle."

"And the something simpler, being something in the order of what you suggesteed at the first, Miss Miranda?"

"Yes, my lord. It would have dignity and it would have charm but, most of all, it would be quite cozy."

"Cozy. Hmmm. I am not at all sure that is a proper term for the seat of a viscount. Not at all grand, you know. I am inclined to believe my future viscountess would wish something of a more impressive appearance. Cozy? I think not. If your uncle is in, I just might drop over and see what he has done."

Miranda bit her lip in disappointment and offered to accompany his lordship to the offices in Upper Parliament, just a short walk away.

Lord Farnsworth said he would be glad of her company and they strolled back across the Market Place, turned left onto Clumber, which brought them onto Upper Parliament close to their destination.

By that time they were deeply engaged in conversation, so deeply in fact that they quite passed by the entrance to Mr. Thorpe's building and strolled on, heedless of all but the tremendously interesting topic they were discussing.

Ostensibly, the conversation revolved about the new house but, for some unaccountable reason, Lord Farnsworth felt called upon to explain in great detail how he had come to a decision regarding his mode of living. This led to a revelation about his ambitions for himself, and it was only natural that Miranda found it incumbent upon herself to reveal to him her own ambitions. There was much talk of the diligence and loneliness that went into restoring a family's fortune and of the diligence and frustration in attempting, as a female, to make a contribution to the architecture of the nation.

Lord Farnsworth found himself in sympathy with Miranda and Miranda discovered herself filled with admiration for his lordship. In fact, they were having a most enjoyable time sharing their experiences of life when suddenly they both stopped speaking and stared about them.

"I say! Do you have any idea where we have got to?" asked Lord Farnsworth.

Miranda shook her head. "It does not look the least bit like Upper Parliament, my lord."

For a moment they stared at each other and then broke into laughter.

It was a rural scene that met their eyes, except behind them where, in the distance, the spires of Nottingham could be easily distinguished.

At once they busily made apologies to each other, and Lord Farnsworth hailed a passing carriage. The lady and gentleman occupying it, when they discovered it was the district's little-known viscount in the company of Thorpe's niece, fell all over themselves for the opportunity to accommodate his lordship. This was a most excellent way for them to gain his notice and perhaps to pickup juicy tidbits of gossip as well. Indeed, they were honored by the privilege of carrying his lordship and friend into the city to Mr. Thorpe's offices in Upper Parliament Street.

Miranda did not join his lordship in her uncle's office but waited patiently outside, while she devoted herself to tasting this new experience that had come to her. The presence of Crenshaw and Piper did not allow her to go too deeply into a reverie on the subject and she was content just to muse as she stared out of the window.

In a little while, Lord Farnsworth came out, looking very pleased. In his hand he carried a long roll of parchment. He came over to Miranda and gestured with it.

"It begins to appear that, indeed, we are making progress, Miss Miranda. I have here the sketches and plans for the house. I am going to take them home with me and study them. I dare say you have seen them, so I'll not bother you about them just yet, but I do have a wish to show them to someone else and, if she—that other party—should be taken with them, there is nothing to stop the work from proceeding. I hope I shall have the joyful news in the next few days. Perhaps your uncle and you would be pleased to call upon me, say the day after next."

Miranda seemed a little out of countenance as she indicated she would so inform Mr. Thorpe. Her response was notable for its reserve, completely unlike her manner of an hour ago.

It gave Lord Farnsworth pause, but as he did not see any reason to be concerned, he took his leave and departed.

Miranda then went in to her uncle and inquired how the Farnsworth business was progressing.

"I venture to say that you will think it is going quite well," said Uncle Sylvester. "And then again not quite so well. I showed him, briefly, what we were proposing and he seemed to accept it. He has someone else whose approval of the business he seeks, so I had no recourse but to allow him to take the plans out of the office. I am not too happy about that. I thought that we could have sat down with them, come to conclusions, and then begun the work. This is just so much added delay, as I explained to him. He merely responded that work could be initiated at once if the plan was liked in certain quarters. I assume, therefore, that he is not going to another architect with them."

"No, Uncle, not another architect. I believe he is taking them to the woman he loves. I must say that is most thoughtful of him. How very devoted he must be to her to allow her word to carry so much weight with him! I wonder who she may be," she ended softly, a strange look in her eyes.

"Are you sure of this, child? How very odd if it is so! It is hardly a female's province, I should say—but, well, I dare say he knows what he is about. I pray you are right, for I should hate to have to go to court over the theft of my plans."

"Oh, Uncle, how can you say any such thing? I am sure that Lord Farnsworth is the personification of honor. Why, he and I went for a stroll away into the country and he could not have been more gallant in seeing me safely back—"

"Eh? When was this?" demanded Mr. Thorpe.

Miranda sat herself down beside the desk and replied, nonchalantly, "Oh, just a very short while ago. We had just come back from our walk when we came in. I dare say we were talking together for more than two hours, although it hardly seemed so long."

Mr. Thorpe frowned. "Do I hear you correctly? You were out in the countryside, alone with a strange man? Miranda, this is outrageous!"

"Oh, Uncle, there is nothing at all strange about Viscount Farnsworth. If ever there was a man to be trusted, he is that man."

"Thank you, my dear, for that wonderful testimonial. I am not saying he is not. All I am saying is that it is most exceptional behavior in both of you to go off by yourself, he a bachelor and you a maiden lady. It is not to be condoned, and I do not wish to hear of you ever doing such a thing again—not as long as you are under my roof, niece!" He ended by getting rather red in the face.

"Rather than see you turn purple with apoplexy, Uncle, I will make very sure that you never hear of it again. But that is not to say I should not go again with his lordship, if he should ask me."

Mr. Thorpe stared at her. "What the devil has got into you, girl? Never think me blind, my dear. I have eyes to see with and I am not liking what I believe I am seeing."

"And what is it that you believe you are seeing?"

"My favorite, the niece who is dear to my heart, about to lose her heart, and to no purpose. My sweet, you are but the niece and the daughter of architects—an honorable profession, of course, but who are you to look up at a viscount, and an extraordinarily wealthy one at that—"

"Extraordinarily wealthy, Uncle?"

"Indeed! The Farnsworths have always been the leading family in these parts. It is the land, you see. They tell me that the Farnsworth holding extends over the richest farming land in the area."

"But he was just telling me how much he had to do to reclaim the family's wealth—"

"But of course, and more power to his lordship. It was his uncle, you see, who attended to the gaming tables in London instead of business in Nottinghamshire, letting Farnsfield fall upon such evil times. I regret to say it, but the late viscount could not have been succeeded by a better man nor at a better time than by the present Viscount Farnsworth. But the wealth was always there, in the soil. It just took a bit of managing to get the advantage of it, you see. His lordship did not move a muscle or blink an eye when I gave him an estimate of £87,000 for his new house. Either he is as fine a card player as ever lived or such a sum is well in his hand."

"Then you think he is very, very wealthy?" asked Miranda in a faint voice.

"Aye, and far above an architect's daughter on every other count as well. Furthermore, you have said that he already has someone in his eye for his viscountess. Miranda, you are too old for such schoolgirlish fantasies."

Miranda's shoulders came up in a great shrug and she smiled. "Uncle, you are so right and besides, I have other fish to fry. Now, you cannot have any objection to my viewing the plans you submitted to his lordship, can you?"

"I believe I could but I shan't. We have not got the final drawings but you can go over Crenshaw's and Piper's working papers."

"Oh, thank you, Uncle!" Miranda said, very pleased.

"And Miranda . . ."

"Yes, Uncle Sylvester?"

"After you look them over, I am more than sure you will have some comments to make upon 'em."

"I imagine I shall!"

"Good! I do not wish to hear them and would appreciate your keeping them to yourself."

"Oh, but, Uncle—"

"And, more especially, I should be most unhappy if you even hinted about them to our client."

"Oh, Uncle, you have given him a reconstructed ruin from Palladio, have you not?"

"I have given him the plans for a most proper mansion, a palatial mansion, in fact, quite in accordance with both his rank and his wealth. Now, I do not wish to hear another word from you upon the subject. If this viscount's lady friend is of the same mind as himself, then our fortune is made. It will be the finest piece of business I shall have executed in my career. It will be my masterpiece, and I want nothing, not even the niece of my heart, to spoil it. Now, get you gone, young lady, and prepare yourself. I shall be leaving the office shortly, and we must not keep your Aunt Martha waiting dinner."

For the viscount, who set forth upon the road for Farnsfield late in the afternoon, the day had been an excellent one. He could not help smiling to himself as he rode along. Everything was in order and progressing right along. He had his new clothes, he had his new house—in fact, it was all rolled up and tucked under his arm—and he was in quite a jolly mood about it all.

If Lady Katherine should approve the design, then he could be sure that she would not take exception to the new house as her future home when he was ready to "pop the question," as Sir Toby put it.

He was so pleased with himself that he completely forgot his needs with regard to domestics. The only thought that filled his mind was what opinion Lady Katherine would give of Thorpe's creation. It was his intention to call upon her as early as was proper the following day so that he could rush the plans back to Thorpe with his unqualified approval and a handsome advance of money to put the work forward.

As dusk began to fall and the familiar country of Farnsfield came into view, he recalled his afternoon chat with Miss Miranda.

Charming girl, he thought, as long as she does not go on so about houses. Imagine! She had never bored him once in all the long time they had spent in conversation. Quite lost their way, they had. Some chap with brains ought to come along and snatch her up before she grows quite sour upon the shelf mucking about in a man's business. He smiled as the thought struck him that her especial keenness on architecture must have driven off any suitors who had found her as attractive as he did.

CHAPTER IX

That evening at the Thorpes', there was a minor tempest having to do with the apple of the Thorpes' eye. Since the Thorpes had had no children of their own, Miranda had had the freedom of their house, even while her father was alive. When he had died after what ought to have been a convalescence, it was the most natural thing in the world for the Thorpes to adopt Miranda for their own. But, because they had always been Uncle and Aunt to her, the relationship continued in that fashion, even though, in the eyes of the law, she was now their daughter.

But at the moment the Thorpes' precious lamb was quite off her feed, as a farmer might say. She begged to be excused from table and, when Aunt Martha looked hurt, retracted her request. At dinner, however, the sight of food was too much for her and again she begged to be excused.

"Whatever for, Miranda, my love?" asked Mrs. Thorpe. "If you would prefer to have something else, I am sure Cook would be only too happy to prepare it. But you have always liked kidney pudding, and this is especially tasty; Cook got a brand new receipt from Mrs. Culpin's domestic. Do try a morsel. I am sure you will like it."

"I am sure I would, Aunt Martha, if I but had the appetite. I am not in a mood to dine this evening. I think I should prefer a cup of tea and a book of Mr. Wordsworth's poems. I assure you it will be enough."

Mr. Thorpe chuckled. "Martha, love, I fear our niece has been wounded by a small dart from Dan Cupid. She was out with Lord Farnsworth this afternoon and has been in a mood ever since."

"Oh, Uncle Sylvester, you make too much of it!" retorted Miranda. "It is not anything of the sort!"

"Truly, Sylvester, Miranda is too clever a child for such nonsense. Why, the gentleman is a viscount!" Aunt Martha turned to Miranda. "Dearest, I am sure that you could not possibly allow your affections to be so easily captured. This Lord Farnsworth is a queer fish, you may well believe. Ever since he first came to your uncle's office, I have been inquiring about him of the neighbors. It is the oddest thing—no one knows very much to tell about him. He is never a part of the social scene. All that anyone can tell is the man is horribly wealthy—but then it has always been that way with the Farnsworths. I cannot understand why it was said that he was not—but that is beside the point. It is foolishness beyond belief that you, my child, should go into a decline because such as he does not deign to notice you."

"Aunt Martha, he is not at all condescending and he has more than taken notice of me."

"All the more reason for you not to waste away to a shadow over the gentleman. Miranda, it is not like you! Now do have a bite of the kidney pie. It is precisely what you need to put the gentleman out of your mind."

Miranda laughed. "Oh, Aunt Martha, if it will do the least bit of good, I shall take but one bite." She did so and looked at her aunt. "Now may I be excused?"

After Miranda had departed from the dining room to go up to her own room, Mrs. Thorpe turned to Mr. Thorpe with a look of concern upon her face. "Sylvester, that was quite bad of you to have thrown your dearest niece into the arms of that scoundrel of a Farnsworth. Now see what has occurred! The child cannot eat. You must do something about it, and without a moment's delay."

"Martha, do rest easy on the matter. It is nothing at all. Miranda has a head on her shoulders and is undoubtedly a bit under the weather. She is awfully disappointed that I will not use her work on the Farnsfield house. I do believe that that is at the heart of the matter."

"But you said that she had fallen in love with the gentleman!"

"Oh, I was not all that serious about it, but you began to make such a fuss that I venture to sug-

105

gest you may have put the idea into Miranda's mind."

"I did that? But it was you—No, you distinctly said that the child had been out with his lordship this very afternoon—all by themselves. Sylvester, how could you have permitted such a thing?" she asked sharply.

"Dearest love, I never gave my permission. You see, the way it happened—"

"Miranda is a most obedient child, Sylvester! What are you telling me? It is all because of you. You never should have put all those ideas of buildings in her head, and you ought never to have allowed her to work like a slave in your office. What will people think of us? We were never so poor as to permit our daughter to have to toil like a peasant! Sylvester, my mind is made up. Miranda is not to go to the office ever again! Just see what such unladylike pursuits have brought down on us! Before you know it, she will have wed this creature! Then what shall we have, I ask you?"

Mr. Thorpe raised an eyebrow and chuckled. "I dare say we should have a viscount for a son-in-law, my pet," he said quietly.

Mrs. Thorpe cocked her head and stared at him for a moment. "That is the first intelligent thing you have said all evening. Now, as the gentleman is a client, I do not think it would be so bad a thing if we should happen to invite him to dinner, do you?"

Mr. Thorpe burst into such hearty laughter that he could scarcely catch his breath.

Up in her room, Miranda was feeling very sorry for herself, indeed. As she reclined, fully clothed, upon her bed and relived each minute of the afternoon's adventure, she was sure that she regretted every second of it.

Truly there was nothing so very special about Lord Farnsworth. He had a very pleasant smile. He was in no way condescending to her by reason of her sex or her lack of rank, and that was very likely why they were able to speak together so easily. Miranda blushed at the memory. How was it that neither of them had been aware of the time they had spent or the distance they had walked together? Why, it would almost be embarrassing if it were not for the fact that it had been so pleasant.

His lordship must have felt something of the sort, for he had not given the slightest indication that he was put out over it. In fact, he had requested that she join Uncle Sylvester after he had had a chance to go over the plans with—whom?

Oh yes, there was no denying it. She was jealous of this other female to whom his lordship must run for approbation before he dared to proceed with the house. Yes, and if she were jealous of that lady, then it must follow that the underlying cause was her deep concern in Lord Farnsworth's direction. She did not care to put a stronger term to it. Why she hardly knew the gentleman. It was just that . . . just . . . well, it was hardly anything to get so upset about. It was really nothing at all to lose one's appetite over and have Aunt Martha all over anxious that something was wrong. Uncle Sylvester had not helped—but then she herself had been the greatest fool. She had gone for a walk with a rather nice gentleman and come back head over heels in love with him. There, she had said it!

But now what am I to do? she thought, as tears began to stream down her cheeks. What chance had she to gain all but the slightest notice from a wealthy viscount—she, who was the daughter and niece of mere architects?

For a few minutes she gave herself over to a sharp pang of unrequited love, until her mind in its rovings settled back on the house. She sat up with a jerk, dashing the tears from her eyes. Of course, *that* was why it had all become so painful! The house! It was to have been her house and now some other female would approve the changes her uncle had made, and it would never be her house again!

Miranda chided herself for acting so childish about the business. It was decidedly schoolgirlish of her to have lost her heart so easily to one who was practically a stranger and she beyond her twenty-fourth birthday. It was utterly nonsensical that she should get so distraught over a house that was yet to be built and in which she had nothing but the interest of curiosity. No, she would put that house entirely out of her mind. Why, she would not even go to the office anymore! That was bound to permit Uncle Sylvester to breathe easier, and Aunt Martha would most certainly approve her decision. She could draw all manner of houses while at home, if that was her wish. What did it matter if she never met with his lordship again?

Oh yes, yes, it did matter! The thought of not seeing his lordship again was too painful to bear. She could never inform Uncle Sylvester that she would not be accompanying him to Farnsfield. It was ridiculous but it was a fact. She was not about to abandon his lordship and his house at this juncture. True, Lord Farnsworth was not for the likes of her, but at least she could insure that he had a very proper house built for him. She was very sure that Uncle Sylvester, following the current taste in architecture, would saddle the viscount with a monstrosity that would be out of style in less than a decade. The very fact that he did not care to discuss it with her and had not shown her the completed set of plans was enough to warrant it.

As she prepared for bed, she wished with all her might that Lord Farnsworth's lady friend would have a taste similar to hers, an appreciation of dignity and comfort in a building that was to be used for a home. As she doused the lamp and closed her eyes, she was still praying it might be so. It would give her another chance to present her own ideas. It would be some consolation to know that the man she loved was spending his life in the home she had designed for him.

Even as Miranda's head came to rest upon her pillow, her dream wish was being shattered in the dining room of the Lovelace mansion.

Lord Farnsworth, filled with the confidence that new clothes can contribute and having the plans for the new house in hand, decided that this was a most appropriate time to pay a formal call upon Lady Katherine and her parents. It mattered not that he had not had a chance to go over the plans himself. Mr. Thorpe had shown him the sketch, which was included in the set, and it certainly appeared to him to be a fine house. If Lady Katherine showed the least enthusiasm, they could go over the plans together. He thought that was sufficient excuse to forgo the turnoff into Farnsfield and carry on to Hexgreave. He never considered the time of day but was in luck, as the Lovelaces had just returned from the day's rounds and were about to have a bit of tea.

He was asked to join them, which invitation he accepted, and he sat down to a narrative by Lady Lovelace of how she and Katherine had spent their day. The earl was not present, being out with his gamekeeper to discuss the possibilities of having a hunt within the fortnight.

Lord Farnsworth had little knowledge of Lady Lovelace's friends, and her conversation would have been deadly dull for him but for the lovely presence of Lady Katherine. Although the young lady had little to add to her mother's recitation, it seemed to his lordship that her eyes held a most interesting message for him.

As a matter of fact, Lady Katherine was more than a little impressed with the viscount's appearance. He was quite handsome, she thought, now that she beheld him in something finer than a yeoman's costume. He could easily take his place in a proper company.

Her glances encouraged Lord Farnsworth to get to the purpose of his call when Countess Lovelace's fund of gossip showed signs of exhaustion. There was a slight pause as she racked her brain for something further to say.

At that point, Lord Farnsworth said, "By your leave, Countess, I should like to inform you of the progress that is being made with my new house."

At once, the eyes of both ladies were riveted upon him. Lord Farnsworth smiled and drew out, from below his chair, the rolled-up documents that he had brought with him.

"Thorpe in Nottingham has finally been able to draw up the plans, and I happen to have them

111

with me. If you'd like, I can spread them out upon a table—they take up a bit of space, you know—but first permit me to show you the sketch. You can get a much better idea of the structure from that than from the architect's drawings, which are covered over with figures of dimensions and the building taken to pieces."

"There is a very large table in the muniment room, dear Lord Farnsworth," suggested the countess. "I think we should be ever so much more comfortable there." Taking the sketch he held out to her, her eyes dropped to it. "I do declare! Oh, Kate, you must see this!" she exclaimed, beckoning her daughter to her side.

Lady Katherine needed no second invitation and was hanging over her mother's shoulder in the next instant, staring at the sketch her mother held up for her.

"How perfectly lovely!" she declared. "It will be a very proper palace. There is nothing in the shire to compare! Oh, my lord, you have exquisite taste."

His lordship was overwhelmed and, despite a small feeling of guilt for the fact that he had had nothing to do with the Thorpe work, he was very pleased at its reception. "If I may," he said, stepping over for a second look at his new house. This time he noticed some details besides the vaguely remembered few stories, roof, and four walls he had seen on his first look.

Yes, he thought, it was a magnificent piece—a palace without doubt. The ornamentation was quite elaborate and the entire structure seemed to be hiding behind a palisade of columns reaching from the ground up to the overhanging roof, which sloped to a mild, central peak three stories above the front portal. This latter had its own canopy which could be made out behind the forest of columns. At each end of the building the roof seemed to swell into domes that were too large to be termed cupolas and gave the impression of burly shoulders hunched to allow unseen arms to gather up the columns as a woodsman might a bundle of faggots in the forest.

"Marvelous!" he murmured.

His faint approval went unremarked as the two ladies oohed and aahed over Mr. Thorpe's creation.

"This will cost you a fortune!" exclaimed Lady Lovelace. "But I do declare it will be worth every penny!"

"Oh, I cannot wait to see it built!" cried Lady Katherine. "My lord, if I am not the first to see it all over, I swear I shall never speak to you again."

"Er—you do not think it is a bit large about the waist, do you? I mean to say, it seems to occupy quite a span, and three stories—more than a few rooms, I should think," said Lord Farnsworth.

"Oh, but that is the beauty of the thing, don't you see!" exclaimed Lady Katherine, all enthusi-

113

asm. "Its great girth supports its great height and rooms! You can never have too many rooms. Tell him, Mama! You cannot know how trying it is when you have guests over and there are so few chambers from which to select. My lord, your new mansion will become the show-place of the Midlands! In all honesty, I must say how much I envy your future lady."

His lordship grinned. It was the best news he could have heard and he was sorely tempted to inform her ladyship of the identity of the new viscountess, but, in the presence of the countess, he thought it would be awkward.

They repaired to the muniment room, and Lady Lovelace rang for a footman to summon the earl to meet with their guest and to lay another cover for dinner that night. Lord Farnsworth would be their guest and she would brook no refusal from his lordship.

Moments later, she regretted having called for her husband. His entrance brought an end to the sweet scene of Katherine and Viscount Farnsworth, their heads together, poring over the plans detail by detail.

CHAPTER X

Mr. Thorpe was all smiles as he nodded his satisfaction.

"My dear Viscount Farnsworth, I cannot tell you how happy I am to have received your approval of my humble suggestions for an abode. Now then, if I may have your permission to begin the construction, I shall be overjoyed to expend diligence and care in your behalf. It is an honor and a privilege, worthy sir, to serve you."

"Thank you, Thorpe. I pray that the business will not be extended beyond reason. I am naturally impatient to find myself in my new house in the shortest possible time."

"I understand, my lord, and you may rest assured that the construction of the mansion will proceed with all possible speed. But, of course, you must understand that this particular building is rather a major undertaking. For that reason alone, it is not a house to be built in a day."

"Yes, yes, I quite understand all that and I do not intend to hang over your shoulder while it is progressing. As a matter of fact, I have been invited to go down to London with the Lovelaces—you are acquainted with the earl, perhaps?"

"I have had the honor of doing a small bit of business with his lordship—a matter of a small pavilion fabricated of Portland stone, as I recall."

"Ah yes, but in any case, I shall be gone for—well, I am not exactly sure. It is just that I should be tremendously pleased if I found my house ready to be occupied upon my return."

"My lord, you will not be on the site to see how the work progresses?"

"I have just finished telling you that I do not intend to hang over your shoulder. Why do you look so disconcerted? I cannot see how my presence will get it done any sooner. Besides, while it is going on, I shall not have a place to reside, you see. You are razing the entire present structure, are you not?"

"That was the intention, my lord. It is just that there may be times during the course of the building that you might wish to make minor changes—"

"But the plans! Is there something wrong with the plans you submitted to me?"

"Oh, my lord, not at all! I do assure you that the plans are as fine a set of plans as I have ever had drawn up."

"Then what, may I ask, is the problem? I am perfectly satisfied that the house, as you have drawn it up, is admirably suited to me. What need have I to hang about while you and your chaps put it together?"

"None at all, my lord, none at all. It will all be done as you wish. If you should happen to be away from Nottingham for a quarter, I do believe that I can promise you a completed mansion in that time. If we had not the necessity of razing the building, it might have been sooner done."

"Yes, as I recall Miss Miranda pointed that out to me. By the way, is she about? I should like to take my leave of her. A delightful girl, most charming. We had a most pleasant stroll together the other day—but I imagine that she has told you all about that."

"Indeed, she has, my lord. She enjoyed your company very much."

"I am so happy to hear it. Is she about?"

"I regret to say she is not, my lord."

"That is too bad. Ah well, will you do me the favor of informing Miss Miranda that I did ask after her? Good day, Thorpe, and goodbye for a bit."

"Fare you well, my lord. I am sure you cannot help but enjoy yourself in London with Lady Katherine for a partner."

Lord Farnsworth did not smile. He merely grunted as he turned to leave—but not before Mr. Thorpe marked the tide of color that rose up over his countenance.

117

* * *

The news caught Miranda completely unprepared. It had never occurred to her that Lord Farnsworth would absent himself from the district. And what was completely shocking to her was that he would do so in the company of the notable beauty, Lady Katherine Lovelace. That latter piece of information was a blow to her heart. As long as she had not known the female that Lord Farnsworth was courting, the idea of his marrying had lacked a certain substantiality and she had not had to face the fact in her reveries. But now that she knew precisely the lady in question and understood what a nonpareil the lady was in the world's estimation, the true hopelessness of her feelings for his lordship were made painfully clear. If that was his taste, the very essence of her dream concerning him was cause for laughter—and derisive laughter at that. In the little sitting room where she had gone to digest the tidings her uncle had brought, she let out a bitter laugh, as though she would be the first to recognize the absurdity of her infatuation.

If only there had been someone else to turn to, she thought. But there was not. In her set, despite her advanced age, she was considered most eligible, more because she was liked than because her uncle was prosperous. Still, although she enjoyed her popularity, there was no one gentleman with whom she shared anything more than cordial

118

friendship. She was deeply affected by Lord Farnsworth and, even though he would soon go off to London, and in the arms of another woman, still she must pursue whatever interest she could so long as it was connected with him.

The thought brought comfort and ease to her. She could do what she had always intended to do. In fact, in his absence, she might be able to accomplish some part of the design of her house more easily.

She thought deeply about it and spent the better part of an hour before she was satisfied that she knew how to proceed. She had not worked out all the details, but she was bound to begin upon the very next day, believing that, as she came to each obstacle in her path, she would be able to find her way around it.

The next morning, Miranda was down to breakfast before her aunt and uncle had made their appearance. She waited for them in the dining room, humming to herself as she looked to see that the breakfast table was properly laid out and that all was in readiness. She stepped back and surveyed it, nodding to the servant girl. Then, deciding that a special note of cheeriness was wanting, she stepped out into the front garden and snipped off a blossom or two. Carrying them into the house, she placed them in a crystal vase and set it down in the middle of the table.

At that moment Aunt Martha came into the room and bestowed a morning's kiss upon Miranda, exclaiming on how pretty the table was set.

"And, my dear, you cannot know how gratified I am to see you looking so well after yesterday's news. It is probably for the best that his lordship took it into his mind to go off to London. You are looking so much better that I am sure you feel quite relieved that he is gone. Now, pray, what shall we do with ourselves today?"

"Oh, Aunt Martha, I have the strongest wish to go in to the office today with Uncle Sylvester. I do hope you will not mind. It is the sketch, you see."

"The sketch of that adorable house? But I was under the impression that you had prepared it for the viscount. Since he found your uncle's submission so much the superior, I should think that you could put it quite out of your mind. In any case, I have always said that architecture has no place for a female, and I was proven right. Now, there's a dear. Come with me into Nottingham. We can spend the day shopping and your uncle can fetch us home after he is done with his day's work."

"It is probably as you say, Aunt Martha, but I did spend so very much time at the plans, I should be sorry to put them away not yet completed."

"But I thought—"

"Oh, the sketch is done, but there is more to a building than drawing pretty pictures of it. My plan will not be complete until I have shown how the chambers will be laid out and quite a number of other things. Since it is my first essay into architecture, and undoubtedly my last, I wish to make it as complete as I may. It is only for a little time—"

"But that means you intend to continue in the wretched office for quite a number of days yet. Miranda, I too know something of architecture, and it is not possible to do all you intend in a day or so. You shall have to be working over a great table, drawing lines and designs forever, just like Crenshaw and Piper."

"Given the chance, I venture to say that I could do it all a deal quicker and a deal better than either one of them!"

"That is beside the point. You are a female and they are not. It follows that you cannot go to work with them."

"Now, Aunt Martha, that is the sheerest nonsense! I have already been working right along with them, and they do not mind it. In fact, Uncle Sylvester doesn't mind it either."

"And what precisely, may I ask, does Uncle Sylvester not mind?" asked that worthy gentleman as he entered the chamber. His face was aglow, almost gleaming from his shave. He expressed his satisfaction with the morning by briskly rubbing his hands together as he accepted a buss from his wife and a similar salute from his niece.

Little more was said as they sat down to a

breakfast of porridge, and Yorkshire ham with eggs, all washed down with coffee.

"And what do my pair of lovelies have planned for this glorious day?" he asked expansively, putting down his cup and then his napkin.

"I am sure I do not know," responded Aunt Martha with a martyr's sigh. "Our dear niece has got it into her mind to do more with that house she is planning and *must* go to the office to accomplish it. Truly, my husband, you did her no favor when you encouraged in her a taste for this architecture of yours. Just look at her! Four-and-twenty and no nearer to a home and a husband. Sylvester, you have got to do something! How am I to hold my head up when my niece, who is in truth a daughter to me, has not the least interest in the important things of life but must go on forever fiddling with plans, when I would have her arranging a flesh-and-blood house!"

"Aunt Martha, that is as mixed a metaphor as I have ever heard!" exclaimed Miranda, chuckling.

"Do not laugh at me, child, because I have not your knowledge of carpentry and masonry. It is no proper thing for a female to know on any count and it will never get you a husband. Sylvester, tell the child that I speak the truth!"

Mr. Thorpe stared out of the window, then he stared at his wife for a moment. He did not dare to look at Miranda, who was bubbling over with laughter. "My dear, I am late. I have a great deal

122

to do at the office today and, if Miranda wishes to come along with me and assist, I must be a fool to refuse. At a matter of fact, I have had serious thoughts with regard to engaging the services of another junior. You cannot imagine how the face of the shire is changing! And I have more commissions than I know what to do with. After this crush is over—and I pray that it never ends—I will sit down with our niece and have a heart-to-heart chat. Will that please you?"

"Oh, Sylvester Thorpe, you are a monster to encourage her in this humor! Mark my words, we shall all be sorry for it one day. I do not know in precisely what way, but mark me well, we shall regret it. Since I may not enjoy the company of my very own niece this day, I intend to visit with Letitia Morley. Will you be kind enough to drop me at her place on your way into the city?"

To escape more discussion, Mr. Thorpe would have been willing to carry her off to London. The Thorpes resided in Basford and Mrs. Morley dwelt in Bilborough, which was but a mile to the south of them and right off the road into Nottingham. Mr. Thorpe was more than glad to oblige his wife.

When Mr. Thorpe had remarked upon the burgeoning state of his business, it had been with this latest commission of Lord Farnsworth in his mind; but after he had been at his desk but three hours and had gained, in that time, two further commissions, he began to feel the limitations of a small staff with a vengeance. He was not about to turn any business away, so he was compelled to rack his brain to arrange for adequate attention to be paid to these new matters.

He had every faith in Crenshaw but was loth to rely upon Piper unless he absolutely had to. Hiring a new draftsman would not have eased his burden particularly, as there would be a period of training and testing before the new man could be trusted to do even as well as Piper. What recourse had he left in the event that more commissions were forthcoming?

The thought electrified him and he leapt from his chair. Quickly he strode out of his office into the large workroom and went over to Miranda. She was busily engaged in scrubbing out some lines she had drawn, frowning with the intensity of her concentration.

"Miranda, my dear—" began Mr. Thorpe.

Miranda shook her head. "Pray do not disturb me just yet, Uncle Sylvester. I think I have finally managed to get a proper front door for my mansion—"

"Miranda, kindly cease your foolishness at once and come into the office. I must speak with you, child."

Miranda looked up in surprise. "Is something the matter? I have not got all that much left to do with this house of mine. A few more days, Uncle, and you will see the last of me about the place."

"That is precisely what I wish to discuss with you. I fear matters have come to such a pass that I may not be able to spare you—that is, if you are willing to work on something that is quite serious. I mean to say, something that is in the regular way of the business."

Her eyes opened wide and stared at her uncle while her lips trembled with emotion.

"Oh, Uncle Sylvester, what are you saying?"

He smiled and beckoned to her. "Come and we shall talk."

Once inside the office, Miranda was full of questions and Mr. Thorpe had to use forceful eloquence to quiet her before he could begin.

"It is quite simple, my dear. This morning, by the greatest stroke of luck, I have had two gentlemen call and each of them has given me a commission. Now, you know how hard-pressed I am for help. The Farnsworth matter is so great an undertaking that it has quite strained the talents of this office. Now I have all this new business to attend to, and I am sure that I shall have to engage additional people if I am to be free to handle it.

"This brings me to you, my sweet. You have got a knowledge of the profession which, in a female, may be thought exceptional, but at the moment I do not wish to stick to minor considerations. I know what you can do and, what is more important, I can trust you. As there is always someone about to whom you can turn for assistance in the event you find yourself in difficulty, I am not averse to put you to work on one of these projects. As soon as the men have completed the major conceptions, according to my suggestions of course, I shall assign the detailing of one of the plans to you. Now, how do you feel about that?"

"Indeed, Uncle Sylvester, I am most flattered—but I have a much better idea. If you will recall, I was close to the Farnsworth matter from its early days, and therefore it seems to me a far wiser course for me to carry on with it. I do not think that you can trust me with these new matters—I have not had that much experience—but in the case of the Farnsfield house I learned a great deal from Mr. Crenshaw and yourself. Yes, I think that would be a far better arrangement. I shall carry on with the Farnsfield matter and—"

"Nonsense, child! What can you do with the Farnsfield house? The business has been placed in the hands of the builder, Nicolson. It is now up to him to execute the plans that we have drawn up and that the viscount has approved."

"Nicolson? I do not doubt that he is extremely competent to put up cottages, perhaps even a *cottage ornée*, but I ask you, Uncle, how many great houses has Mr. Nicolson constructed? In fact, who in these environs has ever put up a great house in the last century?"

"Miranda, I do wish that you would remember who is the architect in this office! Child, Mr. Nicolson and I have worked together on quite a number of undertakings, all of them eminently successful. I have found him quite reliable and knowledgeable in his limited sphere. Now, I would draw your attention to—"

"Very well, Uncle, you will allow Mr. Nicolson free rein in the pursuit of the excellence you devised. I do not care how marvelous a builder Nicolson is, I should always want to make sure that he is following what I have laid out to the letter and to the line. Uncle Sylvester, this is too great a task for one mind—a builder's mind—to encompass. Someone has got to be about to see that Mr. Nicolson does not take the bit in his teeth, as it were, and arrive at some conclusion that you never planned. Now, that is precisely what I can do for you."

Mr. Thorpe looked annoyed, then worried. "I wish you had not said that. Now you have shaken my confidence, blast! Yes, this is something beyond both his and my experience, and I dare say that it would not hurt to monitor his progress. But that is not to say that you are in any way qualified for such a responsibility, my child. I have not the time myself to spare for it and must find someone else.

Nor can I spare Crenshaw. I shall need him to work with me on the new commissions. Devil take it, that leaves but Piper! Him I could spare, but in that young man I have no great faith."

"Don't you see? That is where I can be of assistance. Mr. Piper has a detailed knowledge of architectural practice and I have the judgment and the taste that you and I have always shared. Besides, I cannot go driving about the country all by myself and I shall have to get up to Farnsfield two or three times in the week. Yes, that would be perfect, I am sure."

"I am not at all sure that I like the idea of you gadding about the countryside with young Piper. My lack of faith in him extends quite beyond the profession, my dear."

Miranda laughed. "Oh, Uncle, you have naught to worry about! Mr. Piper and I shall get along famously. Never doubt it!"

"It is precisely how famously he will get along with you that fills me with uneasiness," retorted Mr. Thorpe.

"Oh? Then you have as little faith in me, your devoted niece, my beloved Uncle."

"That is not what I meant!," he snapped.

"Then it is all settled. I shall go out to Piper and inform him of the good news—and you are a dear!" she exclaimed as she leaned over and planted a kiss on his cheek.

As she swept out of the door, there was a puzzled look on his face. "What in heaven's name is she up to—and why do I allow it?" he muttered.

CHAPTER XI

Perhaps the most magnificent structure that Simon Nicolson ever erected was Mr. Simon Nicolson himself, Master Builder. At an early stage in his profession he had had the foresight to leave roaring, belching Birmingham, where even though the building trade was blessed with an ever-expanding demand for services, at the same time it had become a lodestone for builders of every description, cursed with far too many eager, aggressive practitioners of the trade.

He had searched about the nation for a more promising environment for his talent and settled upon Nottingham, a very wise choice. Since his advent into the city he had never wanted for commissions and, as a result of building well and honestly, he had been able to gather about him a crew of artisans who could perform the tasks assigned to them better than most.

Because Nottingham was just beginning to experience the great expansion of industrial activity brought about by the revolutionary new machinery made practicable by the steam engine, the demand for factory buildings and homes, from tiny workers' cottages to the much finer residences of the supervisors and the superintendents, was very much like what was occurring in Birmingham, if on a smaller scale.

The situation was much the same for the architectural profession, and between the two types of enterprises strong commercial relationships were built up, one of which was the association of Thorpe and Brother with Simon Nicolson, Builder.

Up to this time, the two gentlemen had done quite well for themselves and for each other but, with the Farnsfield commission, their business truly began to hum.

In addition, the relationship that existed between Mr. Nicolson and Mr. Thorpe was secured by something more than commercial interest—at least on the part of Mr. Nicolson this was so. He was not of an age with Mr. Thorpe, being a dozen years his junior, nor was he married. As a bachelor of some affluence and high reputation, Mr. Simon Nicolson could look as far afield as he liked within the limits of his level of society. And the most attractive and altogether most charming female he could hope to find who was eligible to become Mrs. Nicolson was Miss Miranda Thorpe.

Because Mr. Nicolson was a very busy person and not given to frivolity, he had never managed to make his feelings plain to Miss Thorpe. Despite the fact that he had been to the Thorpes' residence for dinner innumerable times, Miss Thorpe remained completely unaware of Mr. Nicolson's passion for her. It could well have been, too, that this particular passion could never compete with the all-consuming interest Mr. Nicolson had for going off with Mr. Thorpe to discuss the latest prospects of the trade. It was a matter of first things first with the gentleman, and the business of a Mrs. Nicolson had taken second place in his considerations for so very long that it was only infrequently unearthed from the recesses of his mind and dusted off.

So it was that Mr. Nicolson was rather pleasantly surprised when he received a call from the young lady in question at the site of his latest commission.

Mr. Piper was pleased and proud to be driving his employer's niece out into the country beyond Nottingham. With such a high-flyer for company as Miss Thorpe, he would have preferred a smarter vehicle than the one-horse chaise, a heavy and clumsy small carriage definitely out of fashion and referred to disdainfully as a whiskey. But young men of his standing had only rare chances with so lovely and wealthy a female, and he was more than a little contented that fate should have appointed him her Jehu.

It was a fine day for a drive and, for both Miranda and George Piper, the chance to get out of the office and away from the city was not to be discounted. Although George was some years younger than Miranda, their long association in the office allowed them to maintain a friendly discourse in a most informal fashion. Miranda was diverted and George was enchanted. When they came up the drive at Farnsfield and saw the assemblage of workmen busily sorting out their tools and espied Mr. Nicholson engaged in discussion with his foremen, they knew they would have to assume a more businesslike air.

With a show of excessive gallantry, George stepped down and rushed around to the other side to assist Miss Miranda out of the chaise.

After a quick glance at the busy scene spread out upon the grounds of Lord Farnsworth's estate, Miranda was able to breathe more easily. She had arrived in the nick of time. Not a tool mark marred the face of the ancient structure. But even as she watched, she saw Mr. Nicolson turn toward the building and make a sweeping gesture. The workmen responded with a cheer. It was all too apparent. The prospect of demolishing a structure was more of a cause to celebrate than raising one up. Quickly she made her way forward, with George trying diligently to clear a path for her through the assembly.

Once they saw what company had come, the masons, the carpenters, and their various helpers quickly parted and allowed her to go forward to Mr. Nicolson. That gentleman had come to a full stop in his harangue and was staring at her as though he were witnessing a vision.

"I pray we are well met, Mr. Nicolson?" she inquired, holding out her hand.

He gained his composure immediately and grasped her hand tenderly. "Indeed, indeed we are, Miss Thorpe. What a distinct pleasure it is to have you visit us, I do declare. But I cannot deduce a reason for your presence, Miss Thorpe, and so, although I am pleased beyond saying, I am puzzled as well."

"I do assure you, Mr. Nicolson, I did not travel out to Farnsfield with the purpose of burdening you with my presence—"

"Oh, Miss Thorpe, I beg you not to say so! I am delighted that you have come!"

"—But to deliver my uncle's compliments and some slight revisions in the work, sir."

At once, his labored air of pleasantry vanished to be replaced with a look of concern.

"Revisions, do you say, Miss Thorpe? I do not understand. It was but two days ago that I was closeted with your uncle and the work and the order of its proceeding was thoroughly agreed upon. If there are to be revisions, I fear that I shall have to consult with your uncle with regard to the estimated costs. I mean to say, every little bit of extra business is bound to cost a little extra, don't you know. Er—I mean to say, it is to your uncle that I must address myself."

134

"Oh, Mr. Nicolson, I assure you that will not be at all necessary. It is imperative that the work proceed as per schedule. In any case the revisions will be rather less than more as regards the time and labor required, so you can take the matter up with Uncle Sylvester at your convenience."

He began to shake his head in an obstinate manner and Miranda, her heart quaking within her, belying the charming smile on her face, rushed on to say, "It is merely a matter of preserving the ground floor of the present structure instead of completely razing the building. That is all. So you see, the work can actually move along quite quickly."

"What is this you are telling me? If we save the ground floor, then it must stand to reason that we are dealing with an entirely different set of plans, Miss Miranda. No, I must consult with your uncle."

"In a sense you are right, Mr. Nicolson. Indeed, my uncle has always complimented you upon your cleverness."

Mr. Nicolson brightened at that. "Has he indeed?" he asked, smiling happily. "He has said as much to you, Miss Miranda?"

Miranda thought that she had found a key to the gentleman and responded with a little laugh. "Oh, many times, Mr. Nicolson! La! So many times it is beyond poor female frailty to number them!"

"Is that a fact?" beamed Mr. Nicolson. "I am so

pleased to know that my name has come up in your conversation, Miss Thorpe."

Miranda looked coyly bashful, nodded, and blushed.

"So!" Mr. Nicolson exclaimed heartily. "Then we are to preserve the ground floor, are we? And what of the rest of the plans?"

"Oh, the revisions will be in your hands, Mr. Nicolson, long before you have need of them. I do assure you that the work will be speeded for the changes and there will be no increase in the cost. For example, you must know that the sandstone facing has been altered to large, gray brick and you would be well advised to set in a store of the materials—"

"Gray brick! But I have already put my order in for sandstone, Miss Thorpe!"

"Surely you can just as easily have it changed, Mr. Nicolson," she said with an engaging smile.

Mr. Nicolson smiled weakly. "Aye, I dare say—but then you have just said there would be no increase in the cost. My dear Miss Thorpe, I cannot believe that your uncle is not aware of the difference in price between common sandstone and fabricated brick!"

"Oh, he is, he is, Mr. Nicolson! But when you consider that the structure will only rise two stories above the ground floor instead of three, you can see at once—you are so very clever, Mr. Nicolson—that the cost of a story less more than offsets the difference between a sandstone facing and one of gray brick."

"T-two s-stories instead of three?" asked Mr. Nicolson weakly.

Miranda laughed airily. "Oh, I knew you would be so happy to hear it, Mr. Nicolson," she said. "You do see how much it simplifies the work, don't you?"

"Y-yes—but, Miss Thorpe, now it is most imperative that I speak with your uncle before I take another step in the direction of that building. Can you not see that these changes alter the estimate entirely? We are now dealing with an appreciably smaller structure. Of course, as it is bound to be cheaper I shall have to dicuss this matter with Mr. Thorpe so that we can arrange for a new estimate. I have no wish to cheat the good man."

"Of course that is your privilege, Mr. Nicolson, but I do not see what you will have gained. The thing of it is that this Viscount Farnsworth is a most changeable person and one can never be sure of anything with the gentleman. Suffice it to say, he has given my uncle carte blanche in the matter. Considering how he has already changed his wishes with regard to the new house, he could do nothing else. I suggest that to start all over again with my uncle would only be a waste of your time and his. You cannot be forever halting the work to hold conversation with him at every little change, can you?"

137

"C-carte blanche? Every little change? You call this a little change?"

Miranda shrugged. "What do I, a mere female, know of these things? If my uncle is not upset over them, I cannot imagine why you should be, Mr. Nicolson."

At that point George interrupted Miranda by tugging at her sleeve. "I beg your pardon, Miss Thorpe, but may I have a word with you?"

"Of course, Mr. Piper. By your leave, Mr. Nicolson?"

"Eh? Oh, but of course, Miss Thorpe," mumbled the builder. "If you do not mind, I should like to hold a discussion of these new changes with my men. I shall be back in an instant."

With that they parted company and George immediately began to protest to Miss Thorpe, pointing out that he had never heard of such goings-on, and that he felt grossly insulted that he had not been entrusted with this latest information. He had been assured by Mr. Thorpe personally that the Farnsfield undertaking was to be his responsibility. Obviously it was not, and he demanded to see the revised drawings.

Miranda turned haughty and slowly let her eyes wander up and down his form.

"My dear Mr. Piper," she said in a most formal tone. "I suggest that you make no demands of me. If you will but cast your mind back a few days and consider how very much work I have been doing, you may come to understand that there are more things that go on in our office than you are aware of. Now, if Mr. Thorpe, my uncle and your employer, sees fit to send me out with you, carrying messages to Mr. Nicolson, do you not think it a foolhardy notion to *demand* anything of him? My dear Mr. Piper, we shall have to make many trips up to Farnsfield together. If this is not the sort of thing you wish, then I could request of my uncle to assign Mr. Crenshaw the responsibility. It is quite possible that you prefer a day's work over the drawing board to a trip into the country with me, and I have no wish to deny it to you."

"Oh, my dear Miss Thorpe, I pray you will not misunderstand me," exclaimed Piper. "I have no wish to forgo these drives. Not a bit. I mean to say, if that is what I am assigned to do, I am quite pleased to be of service in that manner. Quite pleased indeed. Actually, I am rather glad that there have been revisions in the plans. It was pure Palladio, don't you know, and I thought it ought to be a little less so. It does not fit the countryside."

Miranda smiled. "I quite agree, Mr. Piper. I am rather pleased that it is to be faced in gray brick."

"A decided improvement over sandstone, I should say, Miss Thorpe."

"Excellent, Mr. Piper. I am beginning to think that my uncle would do well to recognize your talent better. For as long as these plans are not set in

139

stone, I do not see that it would hurt in the least if we made an improvement or two in them. What do you think, Mr. Piper?"

His eyes opened wide in surprise. "And not inform Mr. Thorpe of them?"

Miranda nodded with a tight little smile of anticipation.

"A whopping go, Miss Thorpe!" he exclaimed, all enthusiasm.

"I think so, too! Now then, while Mr. Nicolson goes on with the work—I say, how long do you think he will be in removing the upper stories and the old facing?"

George stared at the building and screwed up his brow in thought. "Less than a se'ennight, I should think."

"Good. Then while he is about it, we can look over the plans for the chambers and see how they may be improved."

"I should think so, if Mr. Thorpe has not seen to it. There will be one floor less and everything that is left must needs be rearranged," said George with serious concern.

"You are quite right, George. I think, too, it will give you an opportunity to show my uncle what you can do with the problem." She paused, looked thoughtful, then continued. "I am thinking that we ought to go ahead with the plans, working together on them, if you do not mind."

"Why, that would be smashing, Miss Miranda!

Quite! I have always wished for a chance to do my own plans rather than draw up some one else's."

"Oh, I know what you mean! Then what do you say to doing the work before we inform my uncle? In that way he can either approve or disapprove, but we shall have had the chance of doing it our way first."

George did not look happy. "Er—ah, Miss Miranda, I pray you will not misunderstand me when I say that I should rather not present them to Mr. Thorpe. I do not think he would cotton to the idea of my having gone off on my own."

"Oh, in that case, let me present our work to him. I understand your difficulty but, of course, dear Uncle Sylvester would be quite mild with me, however much he disapproved of what we did."

George smiled and nodded. "I dare say that would make all the difference, would it not? Miss Miranda, I should be most happy to work with you on this undertaking. And we shall keep it under our hats for a bit, shan't we?"

"I am sure we shall," replied Miranda, smiling as much from relief as from happiness.

CHAPTER XII

The business of Thorpe and Brother was progressing nicely. Everyone in the office, including Miranda, had more to do than they could accomplish. Mr. Thorpe had had to soothe Mrs. Thorpe's indignation over the fact that Miranda was now going into the office every day. He agreed with her that it was not a good arrangement but then begged her understanding of the predicament that had developed. He was diligently seeking not one but two draftsmen—there was so much work to be done. Thus far his agent in London had not come up with anyone the least promising but, as soon as he had found someone to relieve Miranda from the burdens his new business had thrust upon her shoulders and all the rest of his staff's, he would send her home upon the instant. In the meantime, Mrs. Thorpe would just have to put up with the situation. Why, by the time he was done with her, Miranda could have her own house built according to her very own design. She was gaining invaluable experience, he assured his wife.

But Mrs. Thorpe was not happy. "Experience for what, may I ask?" she demanded. "You cannot intend that she should earn her living drawing pretty houses in an architect's office, can you?"

Mr. Thorpe realized when his arts of persuasion were exhausted and he threw the burden of proof onto Miranda's shoulders. Since Mrs. Thorpe knew in advance that she could get nowhere with her niece on this score, the debate between Mr. Thorpe and Mrs. Thorpe came to an end with, if anyone, Miranda the winner.

The demands upon Mr. Thorpe's attention were excessive. The two new commissions he had accepted called for an inordinate amount of his time. Neither Crenshaw nor Piper was, in his opinion, fit to make the necessary decisions, and the latter was forever kiting off to Farnsfield with Miranda. He did not object to it. Miranda kept him informed of the progress that Nicolson was making, and it was satisfying to know that he need not concern himself. It would have taken up a good part of his day if he had had to travel up there to see for himself.

As it was, the Duke of Roxbury had had a complete reversal of opinion regarding the work that was being done for him, and poor Mr. Thorpe was required to go out to Roxbury at least twice a week, sketch-pad in hand, to jot down the changes his grace had dreamed up in the interim. Then he had to go to the builder—a surly individual, completely unlike Nicolson in the matter of cooperation—wrestle with him regarding the revisions, and prepare lists of revised costs for his grace. His grace promptly refused to recognize such outrageous expenditures, and more time was wasted as Mr. Thorpe worked to find less expensive alternatives. It was not a matter he could trust to anyone but himself. The Duke of Roxbury, for all his crankiness, was bound to be a valued client.

Miranda was very pleased that it should be so and she could have hugged the old duke for dragging her uncle away from the office so frequently. Crenshaw was plainly puzzled by the fact that Miss Miranda and Piper were so chummy and had so much to do with the Farnsworth account, but as they did not bother him and as he had work enough to keep him more than thoroughly occupied, he was glad to leave them alone and be left alone by them.

Both Miranda and George were deep in a radical revision of the original plan for Farnsfield, for they had discovered that with the absence of the uppermost story, the chamber spaces were now all awry. Either the house would have to be expanded to provide for the lost rooms or certain of those chambers that were left would have to be subdivided at least once, and some more than once, if adequate provision was to be made for sleeping quarters, dressing rooms, and the like.

George began to protest that this latter course

144

was too drastic a revision, that when a gentleman commissions rooms of a certain size, those are the rooms he expects to occupy, and not miniature versions of them.

Miranda would have none of his argument. She was sure that some of the bedrooms were much too large and she took vehement exception to any room other than the great drawing room having more than one hearth. "It is a sheer waste of chimneys!" she exclaimed. "One hearth to a room makes sense, you see."

"But if we divide a room that has two hearths into three rooms, we shall require an additional hearth to heat the third room, shan't we?"

"Oh yes, but think how much more cozy it would be!" she replied.

Since George could not figure out how that quality had managed to invade the science of architecture, he was at a loss how to answer her.

The subdivision of the rooms went on without further pause.

Mr. Nicolson, like Mr. Thorpe, was enjoying an inundation of requests from other architects, of which Nottingham boasted a fair number, and from householders requiring additions and modifications to their present abodes. Anything that would shorten the time he had to spend upon any one undertaking was, therefore, most welcome to him. As he began to realize the strange manner in

145

which the viscount's house was shrinking externally and the similarly odd fashion in which its innards were growing more complex with each revision delivered to him by sweet Miss Thorpe, he could not make up his mind whether to be pleased or annoyed. He would have taken issue with Mr. Thorpe over such radical revisions, but since the architect never saw fit to come out to the works and since the changes were naught to make him worry that he might exceed the original costs as agreed upon, he kept on with the work, managing his gang of artisans in a most efficient manner.

More than a fortnight passed and the new mansion began to take on its exterior form. Gowned in a dignified gray, it bore not the least resemblance to the original conception that Mr. Thorpe had had drawn up and which Viscount Farnsworth had approved.

. One day, after Miranda had delivered the last of the revisions to Mr. Nicolson—who was overjoyed to know that he need not hesitate to complete the structure now—she remained to sit upon one of the viscount's benches and survey her creation with great satisfaction. According to the builder, another three weeks and it would be fully completed, inside and out. How perfectly wonderful to have had the chance to build a house of her own conceiving, she thought. If she never had another such chance, still she could rest content. She had learned much in the process and had put it all to good use, as the bright, dignified building, trying to rise before her, could testify.

"What place is this?" demanded a voice behind her.

She turned and there was Lord Farnsworth, staring angrily at the construction.

"Oh, my Lord Farnsworth, you are come from London!" exclaimed Miranda in delight, rising and coming towards him. "How did you fare?"

"Ah, Miss Miranda, is it! Since you are niece to your uncle, Thorpe, perhaps you will be good enough to tell me what is going on with my house! That is not the edifice that was agreed upon! It is the wrong color and the shape of it—why, the shape of it is something *you* drew up, Miss Miranda!"

"Y-you do not like it, m-my lord?" she asked, feeling faint.

"Like it? What has that to say to anything? I gave orders to build a certain thing and I departed, having every confidence that my instructions would be carried out. I return and what do I see? I see only that someone has taken the most offensive liberty with my home and has begun a— a horror that I swear I shall never set foot in! Where is Thorpe? I demand to see Thorpe!"

"But, Lord Farnsworth, the building is well on its way to completion. If you will but be patient and wait a bit, you will see that it is a most excellent abode and the interior a most comfortable, cozy—"

"Cozy! Miss Miranda, I find it most difficult to believe but I am forced to the conclusion that this—this petty cottage is somehow your doing. How dare Thorpe allow it? Has he fallen so low in his trade that he must needs bring a female to toil at it? I say, this is unheard of—"

"My lord, it is quite true that this work is of my doing, but that is not to say it is some mere petty cottage," retorted Miranda hotly. "It is a most respectable residence and the plans were drawn up with a strict eye to economy and convenience. A woman has a wish to see a house that is arranged for living in, as well as something to be proud of, for at least a lifetime. I assure you, Lord Farnsworth, this house is precisely that—or it will be if ever you permit it to be completed."

"Aha! So I was right! Thorpe has given you free license to build my house! Well, the fellow is certainly going to hear a thing from me. Where shall I find him, Miss Thorpe?"

He peered over at the busy site and remarked, "I do not see him about. Good heavens, have they already begun to do the interior?"

"My uncle is in Nottingham. You can meet with him there or, if you prefer, I can take your message to him and he will meet with you where you will, my lord."

"Surely *you* are not directing the construction!"

"No, your lordship, it is a Mr. Nicolson, the builder."

"Fetch him to me at once!" he barked.

Miranda started for the house to fetch Mr. Nicolson. She felt more than defeated. She felt frightened. Only now, in the face of Lord Farnsworth's angry disapproval, did she begin to realize that serious troubles were in the making, not only for herself but for her uncle as well. She turned about and returned to his lordship.

"Lord Farnsworth, I must inform you that the condition in which you find your house was my doing and solely my doing. My uncle knew nothing of it. In fact, I hid from him what was going on at this site."

His lordship frowned down at her. For a moment he experienced a pang at the worry that was so plain in her face and he wished it did not have to be. He made an attempt to restrain his wrath as he asked, "My dear Miss Thorpe, I can hardly credit what you say. My agreement was with your uncle, never with you. If, as you say, you were able to hide this travesty of a house from him, then I must say he is something less than devoted to his business."

A workman on some errand was passing. His lordship turned and shouted, "You there! Fetch Nicolson at once. It is Lord Farnsworth who summons him!"

The workman tapped his forehead respectfully and raced back to the house.

In moments Mr. Nicolson arrived at a trot, nodding deferentially to Lord Farnsworth and smiling at Miranda.

"My good man, I am Viscount Farnsworth. It is my house you are supposedly busy erecting. Miss Thorpe here gives me to understand that she has ordered changes in the structure—and such changes, I may add, as I never have approved and never shall approve. What do you have to say to it, sir?"

Mr. Nicolson turned as white as a sheet as he stared thunderstruck at his lordship. Then, as the wheels of his comprehension regained their momentum, he turned and stared at Miranda. He was not smiling now.

"M-Miss Thorpe, can this be true?" he asked, horrified.

"I fear that it is, Mr. Nicolson. I must take complete blame for his lordship's dissatisfaction. I assure you that my uncle is as blameless as you."

Mr. Nicolson scratched his head for a moment as panic filled his eyes. Then, without a word he rushed back to the house and began to call his workmen away from the building.

"Oh, blast!" exclaimed the viscount. "I had hoped to learn the extent of the damage. This Nicolson is no help. Miss Thorpe, you have obviously caused me a great deal of delay in this business;

150

now I must take steps to correct the matter. I assure you, if it is too late and this beastly, misbegotten building has got to be razed to the ground, it is your uncle who will have to meet the charges incurred. Of course, I do not intend to expend a further penny until I am satisfied that I am getting the house that I ordered. I think you and I had better have a chat with your uncle."

"Yes, my lord. I—I am sorely disappointed that you have found my efforts at design so unspeakable." She turned from him and began to sob.

The pang of pity returned to Lord Farnsworth rather sharply. It was pity, he was sure. He had to say something.

"My dear Miss Thorpe, I never said it was unspeakable—"

She wheeled upon him, her eyes streaming and her face all puffy and glistening. "You call it beastly and misbegotten—"

"Oh, but I never meant it! It is just a matter of speaking when one has received a marked disappointment. I mean to say, I had expectations of viewing something quite different upon my return."

He turned to look at the partially completed building. "Truly, Miss Miranda, it is not so bad. Actually, I can honestly say that the building you conceived is rather an attractive place—might have been. I can see that Nicolson has been faithful in its execution, for I do remember the draw-

151

ing you had prepared. It is just that it is not quite the thing my lady had in mind. It was something grander that was agreed upon, and anything less must be a disappointment."

By this time Miranda's square of a handkerchief was sodden and her tears showed no sign of easing their flow. Lord Farnsworth, now feeling quite miserable, snatched out his own large silk handkerchief, newly purchased in London, and handed it over.

He was rewarded by a muffled "Thank you, my Lord Farnsworth."

"I tell you, Miss Miranda, had the circumstances been quite different, I should have been very happy with this house of yours. It is just that the circumstances *are* different—"

"Is it Lady Katherine?" came a sobbed inquiry.

"You are acquainted with Lady Katherine?" he asked.

She shook her head and began to dry her eyes.

"It is early days, Miss Miranda; there is nothing definite between us. The thing of it is, I must have the house your uncle promised me, and that is all there is to it. You will have to admit it was an abysmal failure on your uncle's part, if what you have told me is the way of it, not to have inspected the work. You cannot blame me if I now take my business to another architect, one in whom I can place my trust. Nor—and I am sure your uncle will understand my position—can I be blamed if I put the charges that I must incur in so doing to your uncle's account. Yes, what do you want?" he demanded as George Piper came running up.

"Your lordship!" gasped young Piper. "So that is what is in the wind! Oh, I beg your pardon, your lordship, but Mr. Nicolson has called off his men from work and I came to inquire of Miss Thorpe the reason. Mr. Nicolson is in a foul humor and will not speak to me."

"And well may be, young man. Precisely whom am I addressing?" asked Farnsworth.

"Oh, I am with the firm of Thorpe and Brother and am detailed to bring Miss Thorpe to inspect the work, your lordship."

"Then you may take Miss Thorpe back to Mr. Thorpe and inform the gentleman I shall be calling upon him shortly. My duty, Miss Thorpe." He turned away and strode off to a waiting curricle.

That night, dinner at the Thorpe residence was barely touched. Mr. Thorpe was so irked that he could not sit still for more than a few seconds at a time. Miranda had no appetite at all and could only hang her head over her plate as her uncle went on and on about how he had been stabbed to the quick by the one person he thought he could trust implicitly. Mrs. Thorpe grew angrier by the minute, because dinner was getting cold and would not be fit for dogs if it continued to stand untouched on the table.

"I can not understand it! I just cannot understand it!" exclaimed Mr. Thorpe, unable to contain himself in his agitation. "In heavens name, why? Why, I ask you?"

"How can I explain it, Uncle?" replied Miranda. "It was something I had to do. How many chances does a woman get to build her own house?"

"But it was not your house to build, girl! Can you not see the difference? Lord Farnsworth put down good money for a house to be built to his specifications. He had every reason to believe that the edifice that would arise on his property—*his* property, mind you—that it would meet his specifications to the dot of every 'i', I am sure that a child of two could understand so simple a proposition!"

It was all too much for him. His anger was beyond bearing; he had to get up from the table and lean against the back of his chair as he shook his finger at Miranda.

"Can you have the least idea of the fool this ridiculous business makes of me? Miranda, my child, what got into you? Do you realize what this will cost me? Now I have got to make good on the damages his lordship has suffered on your account. I shall have to pay for the razing of the entire structure as was agreed upon originally—"

"I do not see that, Uncle. That was in the agreement, so Lord Farnsworth cannot charge you for that expense."

"Eh, what's that? You are telling *me*—er—yes, I dare say you are correct in that assumption—but that is not to say that his lordship is going to pay a penny for the work he never agreed to have done. There is the brick facing that must be replaced with sandstone. Now what am I to do with cartloads of gray brick? And how, pray, am I to pay for the work of Nicolson and his crew in removing it? And more, bless you! It will be charged to me, the sandstone and its application, but what is worse, I must sit by and observe another firm of architects take over this business and shall have to foot some part of the bill for their services. I am out of it. Out of it, do you understand! Lord Farnsworth wants nothing further to do with the firm of Thorpe and Brother! Ye gods, girl, I may never procure me another commission in my life! Do you think when word of this gets around that anyone will wish to employ my services? Why, I shall be reduced to sweeping the streets for my living! Oh, the disgrace!"

Miranda was having a most difficult time holding back her tears. Bravely she tried to say something to ameliorate her uncle's anguish. "But, Uncle, it is not so bad as all that. It was a dear, cozy house that I was building, and you may be able to convince the new architects to take the brick off

155

your hands. It stands to reason that they will not wish to work from your plans and will proceed to draw up their own—"

"Oh, oh, oh!" exclaimed Mr. Thorpe, his hand clutching at his breast. "Their plans! Their plans! Oh, how much they will charge! I know—for I should do the same were I in their place and they in mine—and who do you think will have to meet their bills? Oh, oh, oh! I think I shall die!"

"Sylvester Thorpe!" exclaimed Mrs. Thorpe. "If you do not eat your food, you will certainly do so! I have gone to great lengths to insure a wholesome, hot meal for you, and poor Cook has worked her fingers to the bone in your behalf. Now, do sit down and eat, or Cook will think something is amiss. We should not wish to lose Cook, should we?"

"What's this? What's this, woman? You would speak to me of cooks and meals when the world is upside down? My dear Mrs. Thorpe, have you no understanding of anything I have been saying?"

"I know that you are not eating, and with all your talk poor Miranda has not had one bite of this delicious roast either!" replied Mrs. Thorpe with some heat.

"Miranda! Ah, Miranda—once the apple of my eye, now my angel of destruction. I trusted her! I trusted her beyond all others and she has stabbed me to the quick! Once my darling! Now, *et tu, Brute*?"

"Sylvester Thorpe, how dare you!" cried Mrs. Thorpe, her voice going shrill. "There is not the least thing bruty about our Miranda. I'll have you know she is a sweet and lovable young lady. Now pray mind your tongue and sit down! Oh, dear, I do declare, Sylvester, I have never seen you like this."

"Martha, I was not saying anything of the sort. I was merely quoting the immortal Bard, William Shakespeare—"

"Shakespeare? Sylvester, precisely what has he to say to anything? I was sure the gentleman was dead these many years. But it makes no difference. You are taking your ill-humor out on poor Miranda when you know as well as I that it was all your fault in the first place!"

Mr. Thorpe happened to be striding fitfully down to the end of the table but, at his wife's last remark, he stopped dead in his tracks and stared at her.

"I say, do my ears deceive me or did I hear you say that this awful business with Farnsworth was all my doing?"

"There is nothing wrong with your hearing. That is exactly what I meant. You have brought it all upon yourself by not listening to my advice in the first place."

He drew himself up in high indignation. "Madam, I do not recall that you had anything to say to it at any time. It was a matter of architecture that was involved, and you will admit that in that particular sphere you are in no way qualified to comment."

"I believe I know a thing or two about women's place in society, and the office of an architect is not any place at all for a properly bred female. If you will but recall, I remonstrated with you about taking Miranda into Upper Parliament Street, where she had no business being, and encouraging her to follow a most exceptional pursuit for a female. I do declare that I have never in all of my days heard of a female, high or low, toiling in the office of an architect."

"That is not to say that women have not planned houses before this, my good woman," her husband replied. "There are the Ladies of Llangollen, who some years ago made over a modest cottage into a rather ornate structure—two spinster ladies from Ireland, if memory serves."

"And so that is what you would have for Miranda, that she should end her days a spinster in Ireland?"

"Not Ireland, my dear. Llangollen is in Wales—"

"I do not see that her being a Welsh spinster is any improvement!" Mrs. Thorpe snapped.

Mr. Thorpe passed a weary hand over his forehead and sent a look of appeal in Miranda's direction.

"Sweet niece, there are times when I am sure that I cannot say another word to your aunt, and this is one of them. You do know what I am saying and will explain, I pray."

"Aunt Martha, what Uncle Sylvester is trying to say is—"

"Miranda, love," interjected her aunt, "I am sure, at this juncture I care not a farthing for what your uncle is trying to say. All I know is that he has so ruined a perfectly lovely dinner with his ranting and raving that I do not know what I shall have to say to Cook. You know what a sensitive sort she is."

"If it will make you feel better, I shall have a chat with her myself," offered Miranda.

"Yes," agreed Mrs. Thorpe, rising from the table. "And I shall go with you. I think I should prefer to speak with Cook than with your uncle. I swear I do not comprehend how he can manage to get himself into such scrapes. If only he would take my advice, nothing like this would ever happen. Ah well, perhaps this will serve as a lesson and the next time he will not be deaf to my pleas."

As the ladies retired, leaving the lord of the house to stare after them in open-mouthed frustration, Miranda was saying, "But actually, Aunt Martha, it was truly not Uncle Sylvester's fault at all . . ."

Mr. Thorpe threw up his hands, sat himself down at the table, thrust his hands into his pockets, and stared at the wall. Then he got up quickly and went over to the sideboard. He poured himself a glass of brandy from the decanter, took a healthy draft, smacked his lips, and returned to the table. The decanter and the glass came along to keep him sympathetic company.

CHAPTER XIII

That same evening, a few miles to the north of the village of Basford, dinner at Winkwood was progressing in a not too jolly atmosphere. Sir Toby was forced to entertain someone he would just as soon not have as a guest.

Tony Farnsworth had descended upon him that afternoon with a small retinue of servants—a valet and a butler. Sir Toby had been all cordiality to see and greet the viscount after his sojourn in London, especially as he was interested in learning how things went with Lady Katherine. During the course of their conversation, when Lord Farnsworth mentioned he had no place to rest his head and must repair to an inn in Nottingham, Sir Toby had, out of a misguided sense of courtesy, offered him the accommodations of his own great house. To his consternation, his lordship had accepted with alacrity for himself and for his two servants, and now Sir Toby's privacy was so thoroughly invaded that it no longer existed.

As far as Toby was concerned, Farnsworth was all right as an acquaintance, even as a friend, but as a guest he was a frightful bore. Praying to himself that he would not be burdened too long with the viscount, Sir Toby's hopes were quite demolished when Lord Farnsworth informed him that the construction of his house was in a bit of a mess and that the work would have to be started all over again.

Sir Toby quickly reached for the port. As he poured himself a glass, he said, "And I venture to say that you will have no choice but to put yourself up with me until it is done."

"Thank you, Toby, you are most considerate."

"Aye, I am that!" He lifted the glass to his lips and drank deeply.

"By the way, old chap, exactly how is Thorpe, the architect, fixed?"

"I dare say he is fairly well-to-do- for a chap in that profession. I know he is always busy. That niece of his is a pretty piece, though a bit too cheeky for my taste. I say, is that the bit o' goods that has caught your fancy? Since you went off to London with the Lovelaces, I was inclined to believe that it was Lady Katherine you had your eye on. You know, you never did say."

"And I am not saying now! No, I am not interested in Miss Thorpe, but considering what her uncle is faced with, I worry lest I do more damage to him than is justified by the circumstances."

"But he is building your house, isn't he?"

"He was. I am about to bring in another firm.

The man is incompetent and has made a mess of the matter."

"He has?"

"Aye. I returned to find that he had not done the things that we had agreed upon. The house was shaping itself into nothing I had wished. Damned queer way it happened, too."

"Queer, you say? I passed the place but recently. Looks a right enough house. A mite small for you, I was thinking. I mean to say, if you are going to put up another place, bit of a waste not to make something larger than the last—and this one seems to be a bit smaller. I imagined that the costs must have been outrageous, and you had a change of heart or your pockets were not as full as you had thought. I dare say others in the district have been thinking the same thing."

"Have they really! Damn that female for a meddling idiot! No, my pockets are quite up to the business, I assure you, and that is precisely what all the fuss is about. Thorpe was not doing what I had instructed him to do, and it was a greater house that I wished."

"I do not understand, Tony. The man is not a fool. Surely a larger place is bound to bring a deal more ducats into his coffers."

"Oh, he had naught to do with it. It was that meddling niece of his. She was building the house, you see."

"No, I do not! Stab me if I do!"

Lord Farnsworth looked baffled. "Truly, I do not know how to explain it, but the fact of the matter is that, somehow, she managed to build her own house while everyone thought she was building mine."

Sir Toby regarded his friend blankly for a moment. "Bah! You are attempting to pull my leg!" he said with a chuckle. "Surely you are not taken in by such a cock-and-bull story! Thorpe must be desperate to have offered that as an alibi!"

"No, no, it was not Thorpe's tale at all. The man had no idea of what was going on—although I must admit it completely escapes me how the wench could have so bedazzled the builder as well as her uncle—but there it is! She did precisely that and was well on her way to finishing the bloody thing when I dropped by today. Now that you bring it up, how the devil *did* she manage it?"

"Witchcraft is not quite the fashion these days, old chap," Sir Toby remarked.

"Well she managed it, whatever you say. The house stands as silent witness to the fact."

Sir Toby shrugged. "What is the fuss about? If it be somewhat smaller than you had wished, still it is a house and not a bad-looking one, as I recall. Ought to save you a bit of lucre."

"No, no, that is not the point. I dare say the house would be something of a jewel—I saw the finished sketch—but I cannot bring my future viscountess into so small a place when I have practically promised her a grand abode."

"Ah, so that is where it pinches—the gel. And she ain't the Thorpe female and she ain't Lady Katherine. Smash me if I have the least hint who she is!" exploded Sir Toby, highly annoyed at his friend's reticence.

"I assure you, when the time is ripe I shall let you know, old chap. In the meantime, could you supply me with the name of another firm of architects? I really must get cracking. There is so much to be done now that all this time has been wasted."

"Thorpe's the best that Nottingham boasts, so I have been told—"

"In that case, I shall have to go back to London. It seems to me the local expertise is somewhat lacking."

"But you just returned! Write 'em a letter!"

"Hmm, yes, that might do the trick—but to whom do I write? Blast! You do not think I had my mind on architects when I was in London, do you?"

"Not exactly. I should think you rather devoted yourself to Lady Katherine," suggested Sir Toby slyly.

"Wouldn't *you* have?" said Lord Farnsworth, looking unseeingly at the wall across the room and smiling faintly.

Sir Toby made a face and scratched his chin. "I

begin to think I ought to have found some excuse to take me to London."

"Not at all, old chap. Her ladyship quite enjoyed herself, I assure you."

"Well, man, where did you leave her?" demanded Sir Toby, leaning forward.

"In London, of course, with Lord and Lady Lovelace. I say, Toby, are you anxious about something?"

"No, not at all," he replied, falling back disconsolately in his chair. "It is just that I am thinking I might run down to London for a bit. Ah, you can stay on at Winkwood as long as you like, Tony."

"Why, that is downright generous of you, old chap. And here, I've been thinking that I might be putting you to some inconvenience."

"No, not at all. In fact, as you have got your own people to assist you, you will not mind if I bring some of my own with me."

"Heavens, Toby, I pray you will not inconvenience yourself one bit. Do not worry about me. I shall be quite comfortable and, as this is not far from Farnsfield, it will suit my plans perfectly."

"Then you truly would not mind if I were to leave on the instant?"

"No, of course, I would not."

"Right. I just wanted to make sure. Then I shall not linger. Farewell, my lord!"

"Farewell."

Lord Farnsworth was quite pleased with him-

166

self. From having no place at all to call home, he had managed to get himself a very fine mansion from which to oversee the business of constructing his house.

He did not wait to hear the departing hoofbeats of his host's horses but called for his valet and betook himself to his borrowed bedchamber. It had been a hard day and he was quite tired.

The next day he sent an express to his agent in London, informing him of the fact that he was having problems with the new house and would require the services of the finest architect in London, who must be sent up to Nottinghamshire without delay. With the posting of the letter he considered the matter closed for the time being, and he prepared to make a call. As his valet assisted him into his new London finery, he wore a smug smile. He had been worried a little about Sir Toby but, with the gentleman dashing off to London, he could feel a deal more at his ease as he went out to call upon the Lovelaces. He imagined that Lady Katherine would not be overly happy to learn that Sir Toby had rushed off to London without even pausing to welcome her back.

"Oh, Tony, how good of you to come!" exclaimed Lady Katherine coming quickly forward with her hands held out to his.

Lady Lovelace was seated behind her and wore

167

a most approving smile as she opened her fan and waved it a bit.

"My dear Lord Farnsworth," said Lady Lovelace. "It warms the heart to have so charming a person for a neighbor. I cannot tell you how much pleasure it afforded us to have you with us in London. And pray, how goes it with the new house?"

"Ah, my lady, not well, not well at all. It appears that I ought not to have left the spot. All that has been done shall have to be undone."

"Oh, horrors! My lord, you make us feel so guilty!" cried her ladyship, while Lady Katherine looked concerned.

Lady Katherine led him by the hand farther into the room and they sat down close to Lady Lovelace.

"Pray, do not distress yourself, my lady," said Lord Farnsworth. "The architect failed to pay attention to the proceedings and things got out of hand. It was a good thing I returned when I did or it might have been worse. As it is, I have sent off for another firm to come out and do the business. I dare say it does not pay to rely upon the locals. I ought to have got London people in at the very beginning."

"Oh, Tony, how awful for you!" exclaimed Lady Katherine. "Then there is yet nothing to see out at Farnsworth?"

"Oh, there is something to see, my lady. A partially finished *cottage ornée*, one might call it. It is nothing like what I ordered in size, but actually it would make a rather handsome manor house if it were to be completed. Then it would hardly be a place such as you, my lady, would find attractive."

"Oh? What do you know of my taste in houses, my lord?" she asked coyly.

Very soberly, Lord Farnsworth replied, "If you will recall, my lady, before I ever started on the house, I discussed it with you and I was very much impressed with your views. I do believe they had a great deal of influence upon my final choice of house."

"Indeed, my lord, I am very flattered you should say so," she said, turning pink and raising her fan coyly to hide her blush.

"Then you have not a place to stay, dear boy!" exclaimed Lady Lovelace. "Why do you not stay with us? We should be delighted to have you."

"Thank you, my lady. You are too kind—but I have got a place. Sir Toby has had to go off to London. In fact, he departed just last night, leaving Winkwood at my disposal. Very thoughtful of him, I must say."

"Then he must have known that I—we had returned!" said Lady Katherine in a cold voice.

"Katherine, I am sure that it is not any of our

business how Sir Toby engages to conduct his affairs," admonished Lady Lovelace, frowning at her daughter and smiling sweetly at Lord Farnsworth almost simultaneously.

Lord Farnsworth was looking very uncomfortable. "Truly, I do not believe that Sir Toby knew of your return, ladies. As a matter of fact, I fear that I did not put it quite clearly to him. I must beg your pardon, for the business of my house has proved to be most upsetting."

"Indeed, it should!" agreed Lady Lovelace. "I cannot understand it. This man Thorpe has a most excellent reputation. Did you say he was in the midst of putting up the wrong house?"

"It was not quite like that, Lady Lovelace. Oh, it was the wrong house all right, but it was not Thorpe's house, you see."

"Indeed I do. It was your house, Lord Farnsworth."

"Ah yes—but then again, no. It was his niece's house—"

"His niece? Miranda Thorpe? How in the world can she have a house?"

"No, Countess, she does not have a house—"

"But did you not say, my lord, it was his niece's house?"

"Tony in heaven's name what are you trying to say?" demanded Lady Katherine.

"Dear me, but it is a complicated piece of business. This minx of a niece decided to build a house of her own design in the place of mine. That is what I saw when I visited the place yesterday."

"My dear Viscount, are you trying to tell us that a female had the cheek, the audacity, to order a house for herself to be built upon your land, and you did not know the first thing about it?"

"That is not the way of it, Countess. It may sound like that, but truly, your implication is entirely erroneous."

"Then mine must be as well, Tony!" declared Lady Katherine, looking at him queerly.

Lord Farnsworth's face was now red with embarrassment, and he had to mop his brow with his handkerchief.

"I tell you, it was all the fault of that headstrong person! I do not know how she was able to fox the builder and her uncle for all this time, but the fact remains she did—and I have a partially finished house for which I have no desire set down upon my property. Naturally, I have stopped the work and the entire edifice must be razed and the other built in its place."

"Monstrous! She ought to be horsewhipped!" Lady Lovelace sternly passed sentence. "In my day, nothing would have served but that. At the very least, she would have been transported!"

Lady Katherine was still staring at Lord Farnsworth. "Truly, Lord Farnsworth, this tale of yours is something incredible. You know that, do you not?"

"Lady Katherine, I assure you I had the very same doubts, but I actually saw the sketch that Miss Thorpe made of the house before it was begun. In fact, it was the house she had suggested I have built in the first place, so I was able to recognize that the tale I was told had some semblance of truth. But I have no wish to go into it. It is too tiresome a topic for conversation."

"Yes, I must say," replied Lady Katherine. "But how could she do such a thing? I mean to say, it takes some sort of training to know how to go about planning a house. Is this something she inherited from her father?" asked Lady Katherine.

"I have not the vaguest idea except that the young lady is rather quick and may have picked up a thing or two at her uncle's place of business."

"How very exceptional of her!" remarked the Countess.

"She is very pretty, too," Lady Katherine pointed out.

"Indeed," said Lord Farnsworth, "but she does not hold a candle to yourself, my lady."

"Do you really think so?" asked her ladyship, peering at him over her fan with laughing eyes.

Lord Farnsworth, relieved to be past a rough spot in the road, was enthusiastic in his confirmation, so that Lady Lovelace had to laugh merrily to interrupt the embarrassing silence that ensued.

"Then I wish to see this wonderful house that a woman built, my lord. Would you not wish to, Mama?"

"It might prove most instructive, I am sure," said Lady Lovelace without much enthusiasm.

"Why then, ladies, it would give me the greatest pleasure to show it off to you—but we ought not to delay. I have the London people coming up to tear it down and put it up properly."

Lady Katherine clapped her hands and cried, "This afternoon, my lord!—and then you can dine with us, can't he, Mama?"

The Countess found this prospect more pleasing and was at pains to agree.

CHAPTER XIV

Miranda wanted to be there, but Mr. Thorpe put his foot down in no uncertain terms.

"I absolutely forbid it, Miranda! This is not a ball I am going to, but a most serious conference that would never have had to take place but for you. I shall be pushed to my wit's end to salvage my self-respect, to say nothing of how I shall keep the charges down. I cannot expect his lordship to accept the fees that Sutcliffe will submit for doing my work over again. I can only hope that Sutcliffe will temper them, since it will be between brother architects. I should not be surprised if he uses my very own plans to do my very own work, and if that should come to pass I may not say a word. But it is out of the question that you should be there. Now go off with your aunt and leave me in peace."

Miranda felt that, since it was she who had brought this misfortune to pass, it was incumbent upon her to do what she could to rectify the situation. Aunt Martha did not feel that way at all. This was a matter for the gentlemen to settle amongst themselves, hardly a place for a woman.

The strain on Mr. Thorpe's face as he departed for his office in Upper Parliament Street was clearly evident.

Mr. Lemuel Sutcliffe proved to be a gentleman to whom efficiency was a goddess to be worshipped. He was very businesslike and had a tendency to be rather curt. Superfluous chitchat was not for him, and he gave the definite impression that he was not adding to his reputation as one of the leading architects of London by accepting a commission in Nottinghamshire.

After the perfunctory greetings were done with, he immediately tried to take charge of the meeting in the offices of Thorpe and Brother. "By your leave, my lord, I should like to look at the plans for the structure you ordered."

"Yes, we shall come to that eventually," replied Lord Farnsworth. "Mr. Thorpe, I pray that Miss Miranda is not in great distress over this misunderstanding."

Mr. Thorpe looked at him in wonderment. "Your lordship, I must inform you that she is—as am I. I fully comprehend that the only way I can make amends to you for her disgraceful act is to accept whatever charges arise from it and try to cooperate with Mr. Sutcliffe to the fullest."

Mr. Sutcliffe looked baffled. "I say, gentlemen, my time is precious to me and I must insist upon our getting down to the business of the moment. I am under the impression that Mr. Thorpe is to turn his commission over to me. The sooner we get started, the sooner we shall have done with it."

"A moment, Mr. Sutcliffe," interrupted Lord Farnsworth. "Mr. Thorpe, I chanced to visit the site in company with Countess Lovelace and her daughter. They remarked that the gray brick was definitely more attractive than the sandstone. I found it to be so myself and would have it done in that fashion rather than the sandstone. Do you mind?"

It was a partial easing of the burden for Mr. Thorpe. He would not have to dispose of several cartloads of used brick.

"Of course, I do not mind, your lordship—er, Mr. Sutcliffe, perhaps you ought to make a note of that?"

Mr. Sutcliffe was not happy. He was about to lose not only his prerogative as architect to select the appropriate materials of construction, but his share of the pertinent purchase money that went with it.

"Of course, Lord Farnsworth, I shall most certainly take your wishes into consideration, but I fear that I must see what has to be done before I can bind myself to the smallest stone, to the smallest board. After all, I shall be responsible for the whole and therefore must give deep consideration to each and every facet of the edifice."

"I assure you, Mr. Sutcliffe, I was quite satisfied with the building that Mr. Thorpe came up with. So long as we are about to start afresh, I do not see that we cannot make a little change here and there."

"Lord Farnsworth, I take into consideration that you, my lord, are not an architect. Lord Farnsworth, I take into consideration that you, my lord, have good cause to be dissatisfied with your present architect. In all my years as a master in this profession, I have always given satisfaction, and that is only because I never fail to examine each step of the construction with the greatest care. Now, if it pleases you, my lord, I should like to examine the plans. It was the reason we came to Thorpe's, and I cannot say more until I have seen them and had a chance to peruse them. I do not doubt that, in the light of this gentleman's performance, they shall have to be revised."

Lord Farnsworth turned to Mr. Thorpe. "You have the plans?"

Mr. Thorpe lifted the roll of parchments from his desk and handed them to Mr. Sutcliffe. "I fear, sir, you will find that certain alterations appear upon these drawings in a most unprofessional hand. They were done without my knowledge or approval. I should not wish you to get an impression that our work is not on the highest level."

Mr. Sutcliffe merely raised an eyebrow and accepted the roll. "If I may," he said, opening the roll partially and rapidly scanning its contents.

He shook his head and clucked in disapproval. "They are in a most reprehensible state," he said as he rolled the papers back up. "I shall have to take them back to my chambers and examine them more carefully than I can do here. I must also ask your permission, my lord, to go out to the site and examine for myself the lay of the land, the state of the present building, and what have you."

"Of course. I expect then that you will be able to inform us as to what needs to be done to get the work back in hand by this evening."

"I must disagree, Lord Farnsworth. Considering the state of the plans, considering the state of the structure, it will be more like a week before I can make a proper determination."

"A week!" exclaimed his lordship, aghast. "Good God, man! Do you realize how far behind the house is already?"

"My lord, I suggest you take that part of the business up with Mr. Thorpe," replied Mr. Sutcliffe. "I cannot, in all good conscience, promise a determination sooner. If you gentlemen will excuse me, I have work to do." He stood up, tucked the roll under his arm, bowed to Lord Farnsworth, nodded to Mr. Thorpe, and walked out.

Lord Farnsworth stared at the door. "Thorpe, that niece of yours! Do you see what she is costing me? The place would have been finished in less than a fortnight had things gone according to plan. I should have had a fine house by then. I might even have had a wife shortly thereafter. Now I must continue to batten on a friend for my residence and—Oh dear!" he groaned suddenly. "I quite forgot! He is bound to be back and in a rage! Mr. Thorpe, if Sutcliffe has any word for me, will you see that I get it without delay?"

Mr. Thorpe arose with the viscount and promised faithfully to stay in touch with the Londoner. They shook hands and Lord Farnsworth departed.

Mr. Thorpe had the oddest feeling that there was a certain warmth in the viscount's manner toward him. In fact, if he had not known better he would have thought that Lord Farnsworth resented Sutcliffe almost as much as he did himself.

Countess Lovelace and her daughter were seated in their barouche, which was a short distance into the Farnsfield estate on a little rise from which they could survey the Farnsworth fiasco. It was about noon and they had been studying the vista of the partially completed house for a few minutes.

Finally Lady Katherine remarked, "Mama, if I should happen to wed a viscount, one who was not niggardly and who found London a most attractive place to reside . . . If he, my husband, that is, were to purchase a magnificent town house, then what need would I have for an equally magnificent country house?"

"Of course, my child, there are viscounts and then there are viscounts—but I take it that you do not find this place without charm?"

"I think it will be a most attractive place when it is done. Nothing so grand as Hexgreave—but then, if one could have grandness in London, it matters little, it seems to me, what one has in Nottingham."

"I must say, the woman has taste," commented the countess. "I would not care to live my life in so small a house. But then, as you say, if one can have a life in London, it makes no great difference, does it?"

"No, it does not, Mama, especially as I am not at all sure that we have heard the right of the tale regarding the Thorpe woman. It is rather difficult to believe, for all the fuss that is being made, that Lord Farnsworth and she—well, I do not wish to put a name to it."

"No, dear child, there is no need. I have been thinking much along the same lines. I should imagine that it will be some time before this new place is fit for habitation, whereas the Thorpe woman's house could be done up in a fraction of the time—and from the way Lord Farnsworth spoke I gained the distinct impression he is not about to come forward until he has got himself a house."

Lady Katherine smiled. "Do you know that, since Tony has been coming to call, Toby is beginning to sound like a suitor? Though I must say I was very dismayed that he did not come to call before going off to London. I have my doubts about him."

"Katherine, you are the daughter of an earl. I do wish you will remember that, and the fact that Sir Toby is a mere baronet. As to his ability to provide you with the proper sort of life, I think not. Your father informs me that Farnsfield has more than recovered its past prosperity; a Viscountess Farnsworth will be more than adequately accommodated. Yes, it will take a very long time to see this house of his lordship's come to completion—if, as he threatens, it has to be done all over."

"I might put a word in his ear, might I not, Mama?"

"Yes, dear, I think you would be well advised to do so. Now, who can that be coming to trespass upon these grounds?" she asked, turning about at the sound of a carriage coming up behind them.

"Why, it is Miranda Thorpe and her aunt!" exclaimed Lady Katherine. "Speak of the devil! Oh, but I say, I do wish to have a word with her. Perhaps I can find something out."

"I cannot say I look forward to a conversation with the aunt. I barely know her. But since it is in a good cause, I suppose I must."

Lady Katherine stepped down from the barouche and went over to the Thorpes', where she invited Mrs. Thorpe to join her mother in the carriage. Mrs. Thorpe was very pleased to do so, and after the young ladies had seen her comfortably settled with the countess, they began to wander toward the building while Lady Katherine pursued the conversation.

"We were surprised to see your aunt and you out here. It is a bit of drive up from town, I should think."

"Not so far as town, your ladyship," replied Miranda. "We reside in Basford."

"Ah, yes. I dare say you know that Lord Farnsworth has explained what occurred with the building of his house. It seems a shame to have to tear it down."

Miranda smiled and sighed. "At least I had the pleasure of seeing it begin to take shape. It is so rare that one can actually see a dream even start to shape itself into reality."

"How quaint—but I believe it will please you to know that Mama and I both find the house quite attractive. In a modest way, of course. It makes me think that perhaps I should like to reside in just such a house—for a small part of the year, you will understand. Yes, it would be a shame to see it destroyed."

Miranda laughed lightly. "I dare say the only way to preserve the place as it is, is to marry Lord Farnsworth. Only then might one have some chance of prevailing with him."

"Oh indeed, Miss Thorpe, how very clever of you to think of it," said Lady Katherine, one eyebrow lifted slightly. "Yes, I do agree. One would have to marry the viscount to have the house, wouldn't one?"

Miranda's face paled and she looked intently into Lady Katherine's face. "Does my house mean so much to you that you would comtemplate marriage for its sake?"

"Oh but really, Miss Thorpe, there are other considerations, you know. His lordship is not unattractive, as no doubt you have noticed. We had splendid times together in London these past weeks. I would not be in the least surprised if he were to pay me the great compliment of asking me to be his lady."

Try as she might, Miranda could not quite hide how deeply this news touched her. She bit her lip and stared at Lady Katherine. It was becoming too painfully clear to her how much the house and Tony were tied together in her dream.

"Yes, Miss Thorpe, this has been a most charming little coze we have had," said Lady Katherine. "I do think I shall have to have a chat with Tony and make plain to him how I feel about this little house. Actually, it will speed things up a bit if the house is finished directly, I suspect, and that is to be devoutly wished. Miss Thorpe, I thank you for my house," she ended, with a smile that was much too sweet. She turned and walked back to the barouche.

Miranda turned to look once again at the house, a gray assemblage of brick that in its incomplete state appeared to be struggling to achieve the light dignity she had planned for it. She did not see it clearly, for tears blurred the vista.

Lady Katherine had called him "Tony"—and to her, he was "Tony" only in her reveries, so great was the social chasm that separated them. It would be interesting to see if her ladyship could preserve the house; yet, if she succeeded, how it must shatter her dreams! Dreams, they were. Never hopes. Lord Farnsworth could never see her as the viscountess by his side. Actually, she could not see herself in that light, either.

But what of the house? If Lady Katherine had her way, Lord Farnsworth would have the house, the house that she had built for him, and she must consider herself immensely privileged if ever she was invited inside its walls. She recalled how she had thought, as she began her scheme, that all the satisfaction she would require would be in seeing his lordship enjoying his residence in her house. The thought that she might share that pleasure with him had never entered her head. Now that the utter impossibility of its ever occurring was clear to her, it had become the most important thing in her world. She wanted Tony and she wanted the house for them together.

But for all her travail, it would be Lady Katherine who would reap all the benefits. How sad! How very, very sad!

The tears started afresh just as Mrs. Thorpe called to say that Countess Lovelace and Lady Katherine were leaving, to come and pay her respects. Quickly she composed herself, wiping her eyes and scrubbing quickly at her cheeks. It would never do for Lady Katherine to see how deeply affected she had been by their little chat. Then she turned about and walked over to the barouche.

CHAPTER XV

When Tony arrived back at Winkwood, he found a furious young squire awaiting him.

The greeting he received was abrupt, to say the least.

"Farnsworth, hah! You call yourself a friend! You are not a friend, sir! You are a toad, sir! Yes, you are a toad, sir, and it will give me the greatest pleasure to prove it upon your body, sir! Call out your seconds!"

"My dear Toby—" began Tony, placatingly.

"I am not your dear Toby, sir! I am not Toby to you at all, sir!"

"Very well, Tobias, have it as you will. The thing of it is—"

"Farnsworth, you have nothing more to say to me! You sent me off on a wild goose chase, knowing full well that Lady Katherine was right here in Nottingham, sir! Do you know what I have been through? Have you the vaguest conception what it is like trying to find a body in London and she not there? Can you even begin to imagine in what low opinion my lady takes me at not having been on hand to welcome her home? Farnsworth, I demand satisfaction! Call out your seconds, sir!"

"You may go to the devil, sir, if you will not let me explain!" exclaimed Lord Farnsworth. "Now shut your mouth, Sir Knight, and give ear to me!" he thundered.

Sir Toby was very much taken aback at the passion in the viscount's tone. He quieted down, his large face drawn into a pout, waiting for the viscount to continue.

"Now that is better, old friend. There is naught between us to call forth such bloodthirsty sentiment. It is a little misunderstanding that has arisen, and I am sure that you will appreciate how minor is our disagreement." Lord Farnsworth paused to see if he had truly captured Sir Toby's attention.

"I await your explanation, my lord," said Sir Toby with offended dignity, one hand upon his hip.

"It is quite simple, old chap. I thought you understood me at the outset and never thought to explain further. I had no idea that you had completely misunderstood and would rush off to London on the instant. By that time it was too late for me to do a thing. I assure you I should have rushed out after you, but I had this house to see to. In your absence, I have been able to get in another man from London, and things are progressing swimmingly—"

187

Sir Toby's features were contorted with doubt and puzzlement. "Now put a rein on it, Farnsworth, and you might back up a bit! What you are saying is a heap of bloody nonsense. I was sure you said that you had left Lady Katherine in London. I'd not have bolted for the city else!"

"Good heavens—is that what you thought I said? Really, old man, it can hardly be so. Why ever should I have said anything like that when I had just left the Lovelaces at Hexgreave? Could it not have been that in your excitement at seeing the return of this dear friend, you could not be sure of precisely what it was I told you? By the same token, I was in the same case, and so this misunderstanding arose—and there you have it."

Lord Farnsworth held out his hand and smiled at the squire.

Sir Toby was sure that he had been deliberately misinformed, but in the fact of his guest's confident mien and calm manner, there arose in his mind some doubt in his own belief. He could not justify it and he had no way of reviewing that fateful conversation other than in his own recollection. He put a good face upon it and accepted Lord Farnsworth's hand with the silent reservation that he would have to keep a sharp eye on the fellow in the future.

His lordship was excessively pleased with himself for having settled this difficult moment with Sir Toby and brought the conversation around to a subject that must interest the squire—to wit, Lady Katherine.

Immediately Sir Toby offered a toast to her health, to which they drank, and then he vowed fiercely to call upon her at the earliest possible moment the next day.

He was not happy to hear his guest and friend second this resolve and announce that he would accompany him.

Sir Toby was about to voice an objection on the ground that Lord Farnsworth had seen a bit too much of her ladyship already by virtue of his visiting London in the company of the Lovelaces. But his lordship was already explaining that he would retail Sir Toby's flight in search of her ladyship as a testimony of his devotion and it would sound ever so much better coming from a disinterested party than if she had the tale from Sir Toby himself. The idea appealed quite strongly to the squire, and by the time, the two gentlemen were ready to retire, the bond of friendship had been reforged in the fumes of more than a few further libations.

The next day they made their appearance on the doorstep of Hexgreave House too early. The household was up, but the family had brought London customs back with them. Although it was eleven o'clock, the family had just come down and was starting breakfast.

189

The two gentlemen politely declined the invitation to breakfast and spent the next hour cooling their heels in the small drawing room, feeling rather provincial. It gave them time to think. While their conversation was desultory, each of them came up with a vision of the other that gave rise to a renewed lack of trust on Sir Toby's part and annoyance on the part of Lord Farnsworth.

Finally the gentlemen were summoned to attend the ladies in a sitting room. On their way through the house, they met with the earl, who stopped and gave them greeting. He was on his way out and the exchange was brief.

"Looking well, Toby," he said and nodded to Lord Farnsworth. "Excellent reports on Farnsfield, Farnsworth. Glad to hear it. You and I must have a chat some time. Like to hear how you have managed at your place. Might give me a pointer or two. Well, must be off, gentlemen—Oh, yes, Farnsworth, they tell me you've got a charming place now. Must get over and have a look. Perhaps you will have the time to show me about."

"But, my lord, the place is nowhere near complete as yet, nor does it resemble what it will be."

"Hah, is that a fact? Then I am sure I must have another place in mind. The ladies, you see, always in a state of confusion. When you've got it done then, Farnsworth—though it seems to me you've been at it a devilish long time. Get cracking, old boy! She'll not wait forever, you know!"

A wink accompanied that cryptic remark and the earl proceeded down the corridor.

In an accusing tone, Sir Toby demanded, "Now what the devil was that all about, Farnsworth?"

His lordship was still staggered and could only shake his head in denial.

"I have half a mind to go in to the ladies without you," said Sir Toby.

"Don't be an ass, Toby. We agreed to pay this call together. Now let us get on with it."

"My lord—and dear Sir Toby, how nice to see you once again!" exclaimed Lady Lovelace as the gentlemen came in.

"I do declare, Toby Trimwell, it was most unneighborly of you to go off to London and not say a word!" admonished Lady Katherine. "Surely, you could have come with us in the first place, along with Tony. All of us could have had so much fun together."

"Katherine, it would be nice if we offered the gentlemen chairs, don't you think?" said the countess. "Gentlemen, be seated if you will. We are having our morning chocolate, and there are cups aplenty. Would you care to join us?"

Both gentlemen sat themselves down and accepted a steaming cup of the rich-smelling liquid.

"Katherine, you wrong me when you say that I neglected to inform you of my departure," began Sir Toby. "The fact of the matter is that our mutual friend here was more than a little unclear in his manner of informing me of your ladyships' arrival back in Nottingham," he explained.

There was a look of interest on Lady Katherine's face as she glanced at Lord Farnsworth. He smiled weakly back at her.

"But how does that excuse you, sir?" she asked.

"Why ever do you think I rushed off to London, if it was not to seek you out?" he replied. "I mean to say, you had been gone for some time and I thought—"

He could get no further, because her ladyship was laughing and Lady Lovelace could not contain her mirth either.

Lord Farnsworth brought a hand up to his lips to hide his smile, while Sir Toby frowned and stared about at everyone.

"Oh, Tony, how could you do such a thing to poor Toby?" cried Lady Katherine—but her tone was not one of sympathy for poor Sir Toby, but rather a commendation to Lord Farnsworth for having put it over on the squire.

Sir Toby glared at Lord Farnsworth, who tried to look innocent, but that did little to smother the fires of rage that were kindling in the knight's breast. He stood up. "Ladies, by your leave, I would have a word with Lord Farnsworth," he said. He turned and with a motion of his head indicated to the viscount that he should step out of the room with him.

His lordship arose, bowed to the ladies, and joined Sir Toby in the corridor.

"So!" said Sir Toby. "It was all a plot to make me appear an utter fool!"

"Not utter, truly, not utter, Toby, old friend. Really, old chap, you are making too much of a most minor business. I told you it was all a misunderstanding—and it *is* rather funny when you come to think of it."

"Funny? But you are not the one to be made to look funny; I am! Farnsworth, the best that can be said for it is that we ought not to be more than acquaintances. I find your friendship trying, if not downright offensive. Now, if you care to demand satisfaction of me for that remark, I am quite prepared to meet with you."

His lordship shrugged. "Toby, I do regret that you are taking it in this spirit; however, if that is how you wish things to be between us, I shall have no recourse but to remove myself from your house. I shall do so on the instant, just as soon as I have found other lodgings. Now, let me see. Do you know that I have received a most gracious invitation from the Lovelaces to come and stay with them until my house is done? Naturally, I should have taken them up at once but for the fact that I was so enjoying my dear friend Toby's hospitality."

Sir Toby looked on the verge of tears.

"They invited you to stay with them for—for s-so long?" His expression was one of pleading, asking that his lordship deny his statement.

"I dare say, if you throw me out, old man, I shall have to accept their more than kind invitation."

"Farnsworth—er—perhaps I am being too hasty. After all, we are friends and, as you say, I ought to be more sporting about such a minor business. Let us say that we shake hands upon it and never refer to the business again."

"But, of course, Toby! I should have been most unhappy if it were to turn out any other way."

They shook hands and went back in to the ladies.

The talk soon got round to the new house at Farnsfield.

"Mama and I went for a drive yesterday and stopped off at Farnsfield," said Lady Katherine. "You know, Tony, Mother and I have been thinking since you so graciously showed us the house. You know, that is an adorable house that you have abuilding there. It will be quite a lovely place when it is done, I am thinking. Yet, the *on dit* has it that you are still very dissatisfied and are determined to have it completely done over."

Lord Farnsworth gulped and stared at her. "My lady is that your opinion of the place? You did not indicate as much when we visited the site together."

"My opinion—as well as Mother's opinion—has somewhat altered since then. I should adore to reside in such a house—for a part of the year. Naturally, when I am married I shall expect that my husband and I will be taking our place in London society during the season. But it would be so nice to have just such a place as Farnsfield might be, to come home to. What do you think, my lord—or should I ask, what does the lady of your heart's desire say to it?"

Lord Farnsworth was not in a condition to say a word much less respond to her inquiry. As a matter of fact, at the moment he was having a great deal of difficulty swallowing. "Oh. I say!" he finally managed.

"Yes?" said Lady Katherine, smiling sweetly. Unnoticed, the countess nodded approvingly.

Lord Farnsworth broke into an uneasy smile. "I say, how very odd that you should say so, Katherine. I had been thinking that, if the house were increased in size—I mean to say, it is a bit snug at the moment—or will be when it is done—as I was saying, if it were to be increased in size without altering its general appearance—ah, well then, it just might serve, don't you think?"

"I think it would serve admirably well just as it is—or will be, Tony. As far as spaciousness is concerned, you do not expect to be living in it all the year round."

"Don't I?"

"No, you will more than likely spend a good part of the year in London, partaking of the delights of the excellent society there. I mean to say, that is what your lady would wish."

"Would she?"

"Yes, I am sure of it. Tony, I do not think a further thing need be done to that precious house but to complete it—and I am sure that your lady love would feel just as I do about it."

"Would she, really?"

"Of course she would, especially as it must save so much time. The mere thought of how much longer all the work of destroying the place and erecting an entirely new building in its place would take—oh, but I am more than positive your lady would be most impatient. I know I should be if I were she."

"Would you, my dear Katherine?"

"Yes, I would."

"Um, well, I must admit to sharing a similar desire. Yes, I can see no objection to being done with the place. It is most attractive as it stands—and then, too, if ever there should be a need for more room—one's family usually shows a tendency to multiply, hah!—well, there would be no great problem in adding a wing or two onto the structure in the future, would there? Ah yes, I see your point, Katherine, and I am moved to go along with it. In fact, I think I shall have a chat with my man from London—what's his name?—oh yes, Sutcliffe. I shall have to tell him not to bother with a new house but to review the old plans and put them into decent order—or whatever it is that he does with the things."

"Oh, but surely, Tony, it would be more fitting to have Mr. Thorpe continue with the work," Lady Katherine put in.

"Thorpe? But it was because of him that I was plunged into this muddle in the first place. No, I think I ought to stay with Sutcliffe. After all the trouble I have gone through bringing the man out, I should feel a positive fool to discharge him at this point. Besides, it was not Thorpe's business in the first place. It was that niece of his, you know, whose house this is. I say, I wonder what she will have to say to it, now that I have decided to go along with the original. Well, they were not the original plans, were they? Poor Thorpe! Thanks to his niece, *his* plans will never be realized. Bit of a farce, isn't it? But I do feel better about the house. It was going to take an unconscionably long time to get it finished, the way things had begun."

"I still think you ought to take Thorpe back, don't you, Toby?" queried Lady Katherine.

"My dear," broke in Lady Lovelace, "I do believe that Lord Farnsworth is well advised to have this new person go over the plans. If they are of

Thorpe's niece's devising, I am sure I should never feel safe in that house for fear the roof was falling in. What can a young female possibly know about such things?"

"Countess, as surprising as it may seen, Miss Thorpe is rather knowledgeable about housebuilding. I have had occasion to speak with her and have come away very much impressed. Perhaps it would be better if I had *her* complete the house, rather than Thorpe. Eh, Katherine, what would you say to that?" asked Lord Farnsworth.

"I should be delighted. I think I should feel ever so much freer—to request an arrangement of rooms that suited me, say—with a female rather than a gentleman."

"Nonsense, Katherine!" snapped the countess. "When you consider for how many ages the great houses of England have been standing—and I am sure that a female never designed a one of them—I do declare it would be sheer folly to make such a drastic change in architects in this day and age. My lord, this Sutcliffe of London is a man of some reputation, as I have learned, and I am sure that you are wise to trust the completion of the work to him."

"Thank you, my lady, for your kind advice. Yes, I shall speak with Sutcliffe. I say, Toby, would you care to join me in a run down to Nottingham tomorrow?"

"I should have loved to, old chap, but I had the

intention of asking Lady Katherine to go out riding with me at that time. My lady would you oblige me?"

Lady Katherine turned to him and smiled. "Indeed, Toby, it will be my pleasure, but I pray you will not go on forever about houses."

Lord Farnsworth's face turned red and he looked daggers at Sir Toby. Sir Toby laughed in his face and began to discuss with Lady Katherine where they would ride and whether they ought to pack a luncheon or not.

CHAPTER XVI

Lord Farnsworth was not in a very good mood the following day when he came striding into Mr. Thorpe's office. It irked him that Sir Toby had taken such foul advantage of his absence to go riding with Lady Katherine, and he had every reason to believe that Sir Toby was doing it to even up the score.

He had been halfway to Nottingham when he realized he did not know Sutcliffe's direction and would, therefore, have to call at Thorpe's place of business for assistance in locating the London architect. He had hoped to avoid Thorpe entirely, for he felt guilty and foolish at having to change his plans after all the fuss he had made about the wrong building being constructed. More than anything he had not the least desire to meet with Miss Thorpe. The entire business had become too embarrassing to explain to her.

Fortunately for his composure, Mr. Thorpe was out of the office, and he learned from Piper that Miss Miranda was no longer working there. Piper also informed him that Mr. Sutcliffe was staying at the George and that he would be happy to summon the gentleman for his lordship. Lord Farnsworth declined that accommodation and departed. He found his way to the George and had Mr. Sutcliffe sent for.

The gentleman descended from his chamber promptly and greeted his lordship with the information that he had just been about to call. There were matters of great moment that required his lordship's attention.

Lord Farnsworth invited Mr. Sutcliffe to sit with him in one of the high-backed booths where they could speak freely and indulge in something to lift their spirits, to which kind offer Mr. Sutcliffe agreed, excusing himself for a moment to go back up to his room for the plans and sketches he had been studying.

When they had been served their drinks, Mr. Sutcliffe eyed Lord Farnsworth and, taking his nod for approval to begin, said, "My lord, these papers may at one time have had some value, but I can assure you that they are completely worthless. Now, I am prepared to design afresh a proper house—"

"Sutcliffe, I do not understand you. Although I do not have any further intention of proceeding with Thorpe's original plans, yet I should like to know in what way they fail to meet with your approval."

"As I was saying, my lord, they may have had value once, but someone—and I have to assume it was Thorpe himself, for none of his people would dare lay a pencil to an approved drawing—someone has made rough changes upon these plans as no architect ever drew and no builder could ever have worked from. Now, considering how hopeless they have become—"

"Just a moment, Sutcliffe. I do not see how you can say so. A house *has* been built from those plans. You saw it for yourself. It stands upon my land at Farnsfield, and if it could not possibly have been built from those very plans, I should very much like to know what plans it has been built from."

"My lord, you may see for yourself. Allow me, sir." He began to spread the Thorpe plans out upon the table between them. The booth was not large and the drawings were, so that both gentlemen were quite crowded as they attempted to bend over the papers.

"Here and here—and here! Do you see, my lord? These must be changes—but what they consist of, or what they are changing, I cannot make out for my life. It is as though there were two different buildings laid out here. But one is growing from the other, and it is beyond sanity to be able to distinguish where this is happening. Now since you say that the building on site has come from these plans—in some mysterious manner, I must assume—then I am prepared to say that I can make out some resemblance. But I do assure you, my lord, I could not, though my life depended upon it, pursue the original Thorpe building from these papers. They must be redrawn in their entirety."

Lord Farnsworth did not appear to be put out by the news. "But what of the other building?" he asked. "The present building? Surely, it would be no great task for you to pick up where Thorpe left off and bring it to completion."

"You—you have a wish to go ahead with the present building, my lord? I understood that it was far too small for you."

"I have changed my mind. I expect to live in it as a newlywed and do not see that the place cannot be enlarged as it is needed. Of course, providing your work with it now proves satisfactory, I am sure I should call you in to handle the matter when the time came."

"B-but then why do you not go back to Thorpe? He has all the arrangements made, is thoroughly familiar with the workmen he has engaged, and what is more, if he can read these bloody sheets, it is more than I can do. I cannot imagine how that present building could have been erected on the basis of the information contained in them."

"Sutcliffe, perhaps I am getting dense with the passing years, but am I to understand that you cannot go on with the building, a structure that obviously Thorpe has had erected thus far, for the simple proof of which one has only to run up to Farnsfield? You have seen it, I assume."

"My lord, I have seen it. I repeat, I cannot imagine what he used for plans for the builders. I will stake my reputation on the truth of the proposition that the builder—Nicolson, is it?—did not do his work from the papers before us."

Lord Farnsworth looked very displeased. "And what would you suggest then?" he asked.

Mr. Sutcliffe scratched his head and looked at his lordship. "Are we speaking of the building that now exists, or of this larger creation you suggested earlier?"

"The present building, blast it!"

Mr. Sutcliffe sighed. "What you are asking, my lord, will call for a great deal of preparation. To continue with that particular structure, I shall have to measure every aspect and reduce it all to a new drawing. Having gone so far, I shall be able to continue the drawing of a complete set of plans that a competent builder can follow."

"That sounds like a tremendous amount of work, sir!"

"I am sad to say it is, my lord. It is. And I shall have to depend upon your good offices with Thorpe, for I shall need assistance. One man cannot handle the tapes and the surveying instruments by himself, you understand, I am sure."

"Good heavens!" exclaimed his lordship, resting an arm on the table and staring off into space. "If that is how bad it is, perhaps I *had* better consult with Thorpe. It seems to me that as they are his plans, surely he must be capable of making sense of them."

"I doubt it, my lord. But the building is standing, and that cannot be gainsaid. May I suggest that you do just that? I shall stay on for a bit until the matter can be arranged, if it is at all possible."

"Mr. Sutcliffe, you are a busy man. I am sure that you can easily find more productive matters to engage you. If I have got to go back to Thorpe, I might as well start afresh with the fellow. I mean to say, it was a pleasure to deal with him until we arrived at this point-non-plus. You may return to London, sir, and send me your bill." He sighed. "I never had any idea that making something smaller out of something larger could prove so complex! Please, before you leave, deposit the plans with Thorpe and ask him to call upon me at Winkwood, Squire Trimwell's estate."

A day later, Sir Toby came into his library and discovered his guest standing looking out the window, with his hands clasped behind his back.

"I say, Tony, what the devil are you doing in here on this lovely day?"

Lord Farnsworth turned and nodded. "Where have you been all morning? I thought to see you at noon."

"Oh, I have been out and about, old man. You seem to be in a bit of a funk of late. That bloody house of yours?"

Lord Farnsworth sighed. "Yes, it seems the thing will never give me peace. Have you heard? I am having to deal with Thorpe once again. I swear, if he mismanages the business this time, I shall see him stripped of his profession and cast into prison for high malfeasance in office!"

Squire Trimwell shook his head doubtfully. "I'm afraid you are out there, friend. I have been on the bench in a small way for a number of years—I'm a justice of the peace, don't you know—and I have never understood a matter of business to be a cause for criminal charges. Seems to me you would have a civil action in that case. Now let me see if I can think of a good barrister for you—"

"Oh, do shut up, Toby! I have got to think."

"I was only offering my assistance, old boy." Sir Toby was obviously miffed. Then his eyes brightened. "I say, you have not paid a call on Katherine in a day or two. It is probably just as well, you know. She cannot see this house business of yours at all. Says it is a crashing bore and you ought to get on with it. Odd, isn't it? For a time there I thought she was truly interested. If you should happen to drop in at the Lovelaces', I would not speak of it if I were you. Well, I'm off to Hexgreave. Have you any message for the countess and her lovely daughter?"

"Yes, I do—er, but I shall have to deliver it myself. Be off with you! I have got someone coming to see me."

"May I remind you, my lord, that this place is Winkwood, and it has been in the possession of Trimwells for more than a few centuries?"

"Dreadfully sorry, old friend. I did not mean to order you out of your own house. I am just a bit upset with the way things have been going for me, you see."

"I think I am beginning to see that this lady of yours—who she is I cannot begin to guess—is grown out of all patience with you. I say, there's a coincidence! So has Katherine—but in a different way, I'll wager!"

Lord Farnsworth collected himself and put a charming smile on his face. "Ah yes, Toby, you are quick. I dare say I will not be able to keep my secret from you much longer."

Sir Toby laid a finger alongside his nose, winked, and withdrew, laughing heartily.

Not long after that, Mr. Thorpe was announced. He entered the room as though he were walking on a carpet of eggs. "Your lordship, I was informed that you wished to speak with me, and I sent a message—"

"Yes, yes, I see you have brought those blasted plans of yours. Good. Now let us get down to business at once. Perhaps Sutcliffe informed you of his inability to make head or tail of your plans?"

Mr. Thorpe looked worried. "As a matter of

fact, he did, your lordship, and we had quite a discussion about the matter."

"What the devil was there to discuss? He cannot read them and you can. Go finish me that house!"

Mr. Thorpe looked very troubled. "Er—Viscount Farnsworth, I do not know how to say this but the thing of it is—er . . ."

"Spit it out, man! I haven't got all year!"

"To put it quite simply, your lordship, if you will recall, that particular house was not the house for which I drew the plans. These plans were originally for a quite different house, a grand mansion, in fact—"

"Yes, yes, we have gone all through that. But I saw with my own eyes that certain alterations were made on the drawings, and so I have reason to assume that these revisions have to do with the house as it stands. Surely I do not have to be a practicing architect to draw that conclusion."

"But they are not marks, your lordship, and I cannot read them any better than can Sutcliffe!" exclaimed Mr. Thorpe in great anguish.

"Y-you cannot? But then who the devil can?"

"It is a ridiculous thing to have to admit, but it was my niece, Miranda, who made them, and as she is not an architect in any sense of the word, she took such liberties with the drawings as make no sense to a professional."

Lord Farnsworth sought out a chair and sat

down heavily. "Ye gods, man!" he exclaimed hoarsely. "Do you mean to say that there is no one who can now build me that house?"

"Your lordship, I have prevailed upon Sutcliffe to stay on at my expense so that perhaps he and I together can make it clear to you. The fact is that only Miranda has the least idea of what has gone on in the construction, and I dare say that whatever was to have been done rests in her untutored mind—untutored from an architectural standpoint, that is. I mean to say, she is an intelligent girl—"

"Oh, spare me!" cried his lordship, raising a hand to his fevered brow. "You tell me that you have brought along Sutcliffe, who is as helpless in this mess as are you. By any chance, did it strike you as the least necessary to bring along Miranda?"

Mr. Thorpe took a deep breath and nodded. "It did, your lordship. She is without, waiting in the anteroom, as is Mr. Sutcliffe."

"I do not care tuppence what you do with Sutcliffe, but as for Miranda, bring her to me!" he roared.

CHAPTER XVII

Miranda come into the library escorted by Mr.
Thorpe and followed by Mr. Sutcliffe.

Lord Farnsworth's glance at her was quick and
sharp. Hers was steady as she searched his face to
understand his mood.

"I pray you will all be seated," said his lordship
as he moved a chair for Miranda and held it for
her. She seated herself and thanked him.

"Yes," he said, and went to the table where the
plans had been deposited. "Now, I have been informed that these plans are not worth the paper
they were written upon, and yet a house has been
erected in accordance with *some* plan. Since these
are the only ones we have knowledge of, there
must be someone in this room who has been able
to read them. Is that assumption correct?"

Mr. Sutcliffe shook his head emphatically in the
negative. Mr. Thorpe looked at Miranda and
shrugged. Miranda nodded her head.

"Ah! Miss Miranda believes that there is," declared his lordship. "Then I yield the floor to the
lady. Please come up to the table, Miss Miranda,

and inform these gentlemen and myself how any sort of a house has been derived from these drawings."

Miranda flushed as she stood up and took a step toward his lordship. She paused and, with a very hesitant air, said, "My Lord Farnsworth, I do not think that those plans will be all that helpful. I never realized that my changes would render them so meaningless—"

"Oh, this is too much! My dear girl, you have had your head together with Nicolson and he has built a house—or a good part of a house—as a result. Do you mean to stand there and tell me that you have gone as far as you can with it and are unable to continue?"

"No, my lord, I never implied anything of the sort. It is just that all I had to work from were my uncle's original plans, and it took some doing to change them into what I wished and what Mr. Nicolson could understand. Naturally, I had to scratch out a bit. I attempted to make the changes with Mr. Piper's advice, but unfortunately all he had had experience with was one building from start to finish. He had never been taught how to go from one structure to another."

"Who ever heard of anything of the sort!" exclaimed Mr. Sutcliffe. "That is sheer nonsense, and no way to design a building!"

Miranda turned to him. "It was going well enough until his lordship interfered, sir—oh, I beg your pardon, Lord Farnsworth. Of course you were totally within your rights to object."

"Yes, yes, but I am beginning to regret that decision in the worst way. The thing is, how do we go on? I have every wish to complete what you began, Miss Miranda, and neither your uncle nor Sutcliffe here seems prepared to cope with the undertaking. It seems to me that if you changed the original plans, you can just as well continue on and complete them right here on this drawing, so that your uncle can pick up where you left off."

"Oh, but I could never plan so far ahead, my lord. I had to see how my instructions to Mr. Nicolson were being carried out. Only then could I determine what should come next. I am not an architect, you know."

"I know that!" exclaimed Mr. Sutcliffe. "I have seen the plans you massacred, young lady. There never was any question of your being an architect!"

"Now look here, Sutcliffe, the fact remains, and it is staring us in the face, that my niece has managed, without the benefit of a competent professional—Piper is a long way from being qualified— to begin a respectable structure. Perhaps Nicolson relied for much of it upon his own experience, but that happens with the best of us. We do not tell the builder precisely how to do his work. He has to decide a thing or two for himself."

"Bah! It is all a Banbury tale, I tell you," said Mr. Sutcliffe. "No house was ever constructed in such a slipshod manner!"

"Gentlemen, gentlemen, this is not getting my house any closer to being built!" Lord Farnsworth loudly intervened. "I do not give a damn what manner is followed in the pursuit of this undertaking, just so long as it is pursued successfully. Miss Miranda, I beg you to come up and glance at the drawings. You have seen in what state the building was left after I called Nicolson away from it. I pray you will search your memory for your last instructions to him and consider what your next might have been. Perhaps then these gentlemen will be able to understand the process by which your house was being erected."

"If it please you, my lord," said Miranda quietly. She came up to the drawings, which Lord Farnsworth unrolled and held down for her.

She began to study the diagrams, but had to stop. "My lord, the lamp does not shed sufficient light for me to see what I have done."

As Mr. Thorpe picked up the lamp and held it close, Mr. Sutcliffe muttered, "It will take more than a lamp to shed light upon that mess of hentracks!"

He was hushed immediately by both of the other gentlemen. Miranda went on with her examination unperturbed.

"Ah yes, here it is. Now I recall. I was about to do the roof, my lord. I was trying to work out how to fit it on the house, you see—"

"Fit the roof on the house? Ye gods!" exclaimed Mr. Sutcliffe, while even Mr. Thorpe stared at his niece in consternation.

Miranda turned to the Londoner. "Yes, Mr. Sutcliffe," she said. "I was quite taken with my Uncle Sylvester's pediment and wished to set it down upon the house, but you see it was quite difficult to determine how it should go. It is a question of how many layers of bricks must go before—"

"Courses, Miss Thorpe—courses, not layers," interposed Mr. Sutcliffe. "We can at least make the pretense of being architects by using the appropriate terms, I pray."

"Very well, Mr. Sutcliffe. I did not know how many courses of bricks should intervene before the roof was laid on—"

"But you do not lay on a roof like a hat, Miss Thorpe!" protested Mr. Sutcliffe.

"Sutcliffe, will you be silent!" interjected Lord Farnsworth. "I will say this for Miss Miranda's language: I do understand what she is driving at. I pray you will have patience; you will gain comprehension, too. Pray proceed, Miss Miranda," he urged.

"My lord, to my way of thinking it is very much like putting on a hat. I mean to say, if you do not put sufficient layers—er, courses—on before the

214

pediment begins, the structure will have a beet-ling look—very much like a chap with his hat drawn down upon his face, and that is sullen and morose, don't you think?"

"Of course I do. I understand perfectly," his lordship assured her.

"Thank you, my lord. Well then, I did not think one could try on a course of bricks like one could try on a hat, so I bethought myself it was time to attempt to do it by sketching the appear-ance of the building with a varied number of courses until I found the right number to preserve the airy aspect that I loved. I regret to say, my lord, that was to be the very next bit of work I had scheduled when you brought the matter to a halt."

"I see. But you could go on with it now?"

"Oh, I should dearly love to see it completed. I could prepare the sketches in a day, I am sure."

"Then do—"

"My Lord Farnsworth, I must protest!" inter-posed Mr. Sutcliffe. He stood up now and came forward to the table. "May I point out, sir, that in this room are two gentlemen boasting competence as finished architects of a high degree. I have no doubt but that my colleague will support me when I herewith declare this is all stuff and non-sense! One does not build a building as though one were fitting oneself out with a new suit of clothing. Sir, we are not tailors! A house cannot be fitted. We have got to start from the ground up—

but, before we begin, we have got to know precisely what to tell the builder to do. And that, my lord, if I am not trying your comprehension, must concern the structure as a whole. After all, the foundation has got to support all that is laid upon it. I direct your attention to the fallacy of Miss Thorpe's approach in this instance. Having decided upon the number of courses, how does Miss Thorpe plan to do the ceilings of that upper story? Their height is bound to be affected by the loftiness or lack thereof of the roof she intends to fit upon this construction."

"Sutcliffe, there is no call for your remarks and you know it," retorted Mr. Thorpe. "The child has done exceedingly well as far as she has gone, you must admit. Now then, Miranda, please inform his lordship how you intended to deal with the ceilings."

Miranda blushed as she shook her head. "I fear that I had no solution for that problem. I had hoped that perhaps Mr. Nicolson might suggest something, or that even Piper would manage to come up with an idea. I knew that it would have to be considered, but I was praying the ceilings would come to a reasonable height under the roof."

"There! What have I been saying!" cried Mr. Sutcliffe. "This is all utter nonsense! My lord, I offered my services to my colleague in the hope that something could be made of this mess. Nothing can. As my advice would be to raze the building to the ground and start over, unhampered by the young lady's questionable talent, my services are not required. Mr. Thorpe can certainly handle the business as well as anyone."

"Thank you, Mr. Sutcliffe, for your view of the situation," said the viscount. "You are excused and I shall expect your bill. Good day, sir!"

Mr. Sutcliffe nodded. The viscount rang for a footman and the gentleman from London followed the man out of the chamber.

For a moment the little group in the library stared at each other. Then both Miranda's and Mr. Thorpe's gazes settled upon the viscount.

He smiled at them. "I do believe the air is a bit clearer for Sutcliffe's absence," he said. "Perhaps now we can proceed with the matter before us and determine how best to bring the house to completion." He ended by looking at Miranda.

Miranda was too confused to speak and she looked at her uncle. Mr. Thorpe took a step forward. "My lord, it begins to appear that we have little choice," he said. "If it is the present house you desire, much though my sympathies remain with Sutcliffe, I feel that we shall have to trust in my niece's methods. You see, my lord, there are no plans for this house that she was having built and—and, well, without plans, my lord, we do not have anything at all, do we?—except whatever it is that Miranda's imagination will produce."

"I am forced to agree, Thorpe," said the viscount. "But I was thinking that now you might be able to work along with her so that there will not be any sort of sticking places, such as a roof that does not quite fit and ceilings that may or may not be appropriate. I mean to say, now that we recognize that some sort of special house is being erected, we must do all we can to expedite the process, even if it is not quite according to the practices and procedures of your profession."

Mr. Thorpe smiled. "My lord, it would be my devout pleasure to do so. Er—I must inform you, however, that since it is a substantially smaller dwelling that we are now putting together, I shall have to enter into conversations with Nicolson with an eye to reducing the price that we agreed upon between your lordship and myself. Naturally it will be less—"

"Quite—but do not let it interfere with the work. I am sure that we shall reach an amicable settlement, just so long as that infernal house is done. I am not pleased to have to cool my heels in this place for God knows how long. There must be a limit to the squire's hospitality, you know."

"Of course, my lord. I shall take charge of everything, and I do assure you, every detail will gain my closest scrutiny. I am mindful that I failed in my duty to you ere this and would be mortified if it were to happen again."

Miranda was smiling and biting her lip to keep

from chuckling in exultation. No other thought was in her mind but that she was to be allowed to complete her house.

"Miss Miranda," said Lord Farnsworth, "I would have you understand that, indeed, I am more than pleased with your house and have been since I first saw the sketches that you had made of it. Now that my lady has expressed her pleasure in it, I am doubly pleased as you can well imagine. I pray that you will work with your uncle on it and make us all proud of the effort."

The happy look on Miranda's face faded. "My Lord Viscount," she said soberly, "as it will be the work of my uncle, you may rest assured that the work will be done promptly and expeditiously. If all is settled, I beg your permission to withdraw."

A slight frown tinged his lordship's brow as he assented and escorted uncle and niece out of the house. He stood watching them join Mr. Sutcliffe in the carriage and drive off.

The frown was still on his forehead as he turned back into the house.

"I am sure that I did not say anything the least discouraging," he murmured. He gave himself a little shake as though to ward off a chill.

For Miranda, what should have been a most joyful occasion had been transformed into a distressing one. Being able to go ahead with the house, completely free to accomplish her design;

not having to evade her uncle's interest in what she was doing; being free to consult with him on those particular sticking places in the construction—all these liberties, once prominent in her dreams but absent in her work, were now hers to enjoy.

As she sat huddled in a corner of the carriage while her uncle and Mr. Sutcliffe reviewed the situation, she tried hard to revive the enthusiasm she had had for the house at Farnsfield. It ought to have been quite easy. She now possessed every freedom she could have wished. Just like a full-fledged architect, what she proposed was what Mr. Nicolson was bound to execute. She would not need to employ those subterfuges required to convince the builder that she was simply relaying her uncle's instructions to him. Why, Uncle Sylvester would now be in the position of having to relay *her* wishes in the matter! Certainly that thought ought to have filled her breast with the greatest satisfaction—but it did not.

Instead, she was plunged into unhappiness. Tony could call it her house all day long and it would make no whit of difference. It was not her house and it never would be. It was going to be Lady Katherine's house, and she had to build the house she loved for another woman. Bad as that was, the situation was made even worse by the fact that that woman suspected, and rightly, the true reason behind Miranda's interest. The house was a token of her feeling for Tony. It was to have been the signal of something personal between them.

Oh, how utterly foolish of her! she thought as she squirmed in her seat, suffering the embarrassment of one whose precious secret has been discovered.

Her lips tightened; she resolved to have nothing further to do with the house. Her eyes flashed as she pictured herself refusing Tony's impassioned plea to continue with it for his sake.

Just as quickly, her face relaxed into sadness as she admitted to herself that she had no choice but to continue with it. No matter how she felt about it, Uncle Sylvester was now fully responsible for the effort and she would do him irreparable damage were she to withdraw from the undertaking. Then, too, she had no reason to cause Tony annoyance. He had no idea of her feelings for him. He had no reason to assume that the daughter and niece of architects should aspire to become his viscountess. Yes, that was the silliest notion of them all! Miranda Thorpe, who had been on the shelf for too many years, was in no position to look above herself. She would be lucky to find her heart's desire in a tradesman or a merchant, as Aunt Martha was constantly urging her to do.

CHAPTER XVIII

Mr. Sutcliffe was convinced that he had been attempting to deal with a parcel of fools and was relieved to have seen the last of them. He had no wish to dally and, peremptorily, refused Mr. Thorpe's invitation to sup with him. Instead, he raced back to his lodgings, threw all his clothes into his portmanteau, and caught the very next stage for London.

Mr. Thorpe was not very sorry to see him depart. He would have liked to have an opportunity to sit and chat with Sutcliffe. He might have picked up a pointer or two with regard to the latest creations of the fashionable architects of the day. But, on balance, he was more than a little relieved with the way things had turned out. Instead of having to face bankruptcy, he had gained another chance. The financial arrangements that would now be drawn up, although they might reduce the amount of his fee because of the smaller building that was contemplated, were still better than being saddled with a bill for what might have amounted to an entire great dwelling.

Moreover, he was proud of his niece and anxious to get started with her on the Farnsfield house. He loved her and this opportunity to work with her, despite the fact that she was a woman, gave promise of proving to be a most interesting experience. Actually, he was curious to see how she managed the business.

Lord Farnsworth, too, was now able to sleep easier. He was very pleased with himself. It seemed to him that he had pulled a brilliant victory from the jaws of defeat in the person of Sutcliffe of London. The man had been most discouraging in his manner and particularly obtuse with regard to finding a decent way out of the mess. Yes, it might appear strange to others that he, a viscount, should have recourse to so odd an architect, but he had seen Miranda's sketch and he had seen how well, with the help of Nicolson, she had thus far executed a structure that caught the very spirit of her drawing.

The more he thought about it, the more he was pleased that it was her house that was to be his. It was just the sort of place that he would have selected for himself. Only Lady Katherine's original desire for something grander had led him to accept Thorpe's offering. Ah, her ladyship was such a sweet person! That she should have found this house desirable spoke volumes to him of the sweet character she possessed.

But, upon sober consideration, he dare not leave things to Miss Miranda completely. That had been his first mistake. He must make sure that the work progressed as planned from day to day. Therefore, he would have to make frequent visits to the site to inspect the work. Yes, that would not be a bad idea, he thought. It would give him a chance to chat with Miss Miranda. He recalled having had a most enjoyable walk with her. He would be immensely interested in observing how she went about building this building of his.

Sir Toby, upon hearing that construction was to proceed on his friend's house and that Tony would have to spend time at Farnsfield to see that the work went well, was rather pleased as well. Lady Katherine had shown a most disconcerting propensity of late for introducing Tony into their conversations. As long as that was as far as it went, he was not too worried, and it stood to reason that Tony's preoccupation with his house must keep him a subject of conversation rather than a rival. On balance, Sir Toby, too, was pleased with the news.

Lady Katherine was of two minds when Tony came to call and broke the news to her that he would be a bit tied down by the work at Farnsfield. She was immediately displeased by the fact that she was seeing so little of him at present and that the situation was not going to improve for some time. Upon further consideration, she was highly annoyed by the fact that Miss Thorpe was going to be seeing a great deal of Tony. That she did not care for at all. At the same time, she was eaten up with curiosity to see for herself how Miss Thorpe, a mere female, could pretend to build a house. The solution to her problems came instantaneously.

"Tony, dear, why do you not take me along with you when you go to Farnsfield? I am sure it would be most diverting to see how the house grows from day to day."

"I say, would you really like that?" he asked. "I assure you, I would have offered if I had had any idea that that sort of thing would interest you."

"After all, dear man," she said, as she playfully tapped his shoulder with her fan, "I have hopes of being invited into it one day after it is finished."

"My lady, I do asssure you that you shall be the very first to see it once it has been completed."

She put on a sad face. "Oh, Tony, how you do toy with me! I could not possibly be the first when that honor must go to Miss Thorpe. She is bound to be the first to see it."

Tony laughed. "I dare say. Permit me to qualify it, my lady. You shall be the first of my friends to see it."

"And is not Miss Thorpe numbered amongst your friends?" she asked.

"If you were to make a point of the issue, I imagine that, yes, Miss Thorpe might be accounted a friend—as much as her uncle at least. But that is in the way of trade, don't you see. I do not think it counts."

"Oh, Tony, do not think you can hide it!" she replied with a challenging laugh.

He frowned and felt a warm tide rise up over his cheeks.

"There! You are blushing, my dear," she continued. "How very interesting—interesting especially in light of the news my lady mother heard that you and she—Miss Thorpe, that is—were seen walking together beyond the limits of Nottingham one day. And you say she is merely a person you are acquainted with because of the trade? I hardly think so. If that were true, I am sure you would never have allowed such a person to build you a house when you could have had Sutcliffe of London. Tony, are you quite mad? You had the gentleman here and yet you refused to engage him! I tell you that the countess could not believe her ears when she heard—and Papa shook his head in sheer astonishment."

"Lady Katherine, if that is what you wish to think of me, I cannot stop you—nor can I dictate the opinions of the earl or the countess."

"Oh, Tony!" she cried, a little hastily. "Do you not know when I am having you on? Of course, it is quite understandable! Miss Thorpe designed the house and matters have gone so far that it would be foolhardy to entrust its completion to anyone else. Do you see that I truly comprehend? It is just that people are bound to talk, because it is such an unusual case. I do not think it would hurt the situation at all if I were to join you on your visits to Farnsfield."

"But of course, Katherine. I feel an out-and-out chucklehead for not having understood you. I should be delighted to have you accompany me every now and again—"

"Oh, but I mean to come with you each time, Tony!"

"But, my dear lady, that would not be at all convenient. I shall have to go tramping about the building to see what has been done and how it is going. You would have to stay in the carriage for the longest times."

"Tony, I begin to suspect that you do not want me along."

"Katherine, I never—"

"It seems to me that if Miss Thorpe can go tramping about the building with you, then I can, too!"

"But she is not a lady—she is not so fine as you, Katherine. I could never picture you engaging in such an unfeminine pursuit."

A smile beamed on her ladyship's countenance. For the first time in this short conversation she appeared to be at ease. "Ah, how nice of you to say so, Tony. Yes, you are quite right. I am sure that I would not be at all comfortable out there.

As you said, every now and again will be quite sufficient."

As the matter had been settled so amicably and as his lordship had nothing to occupy him at the moment, he gladly accepted Lady Katherine's invitation to drive her mother and herself into Nottingham to do some shopping.

The next day the viscount received a formal note from Mr. Thorpe informing him that the work was being resumed and inviting him to inspect its progress at his pleasure and convenience.

Tony did not pause but went right out to Farnsfield. Mr. Thorpe gave him cordial welcome but was a little taken aback at the look of disapproval that marred the viscount's features.

"My lord, can something be amiss already?" inquired the architect.

"As a matter of fact, there is," Lord Farnsworth replied. "I understood that it was to be Miss Miranda who would conduct the work, yet I do not see her anywhere."

Mr. Thorpe let out a laugh of relief. "My lord, I assure you she is doing just that, but it is hardly necesary that she be on the spot—"

"Why do *you* find it necessary, then?"

"My lord, it would not be at all the thing! A lady to be associating with the rough laborers? It is not to be thought of!"

"But I was advised that that is precisely what she had been doing."

"I assure you, my lord, it was not with my permission."

"Then, pray, how am I to converse with her if she is not here?"

"You wish to converse with Miranda, my lord?"

"She is the architect, is she not? If I am to confer with my architect, I have to converse with her—or him, as the case may be."

There was a look of uncertainty in Mr. Thorpe's eye. "If that is all it is," he said, "I should be only too happy to relay to her any comments or suggestions you wish to make."

"Nonsense! I am sure I can make myself quite plain. I would speak to Miss Miranda about the house. Where the devil is she?"

"She is hard at work on the next phase of the construction, back in Nottingham in my office, your lordship."

"Blast! There's the trouble with having a female for an architect. I was in town but yesterday. I dare say I shall have to go down again today."

"But, your lordship, it will be dusk when you return."

"Be at ease, Thorpe, I can find my way." He waved a hand at the building. "All this means nothing to me. I should much rather hear from her lips how the business goes."

"I shall be happy to accompany you back to the office, my lord."

"Very well! Get in!" snapped Lord Farnsworth.

"Oh, but I have my own carriage—"

"I am not about to eat your dust and I see no reason why you must eat mine. You can ride with me and have your carriage sent back."

"Very good, my lord. If I may have but a moment to say a word to Nicolson . . ."

The ride into Nottingham left Mr. Thorpe more upset at its end in Upper Parliament Street than he had been at its beginning at Farnsfield. They did not discuss the house, as he thought they would, but rather its architect. Mr. Thorpe was no man of the world, but he understood its ways—and the idea of a wealthy viscount exhibiting great curiosity as to how his pretty niece came to be so interested in housebuilding set a worm of worry gnawing at his composure.

But he was not discomfited for very long thereafter. The viscount accompanied him into the building, where they discovered Miranda conferring with Mr. Crenshaw and Mr. Piper.

Hearing them enter the office, she turned with a bright smile to greet her uncle, but it quickly faded when she saw his company.

"Ah Miss Miranda, there you are," said Lord Farnsworth. "I have brought your uncle home to you. I am so pleased that we have started on the house. Well, I must be off now! A most pleasant day to you." He clapped his hat back on his head and left the office.

"Bless my soul!" exclaimed Mr. Thorpe, staring after him.

"What is it, Uncle Sylvester? You look so startled," said Miranda.

"I should hope to say so! I cannot make out his lordship's going off like that. Is the man demented?"

Miranda frowned and took hold of his arm. "Uncle, I do believe that you have been working too hard. Have you had a bite to eat? There is still some tea in the pot. Why do you not sit down for a spell and let me get you a cup?"

"Never mind, never mind. Come into the office with me, my dear—and yes, I could do with a spot of tea. Fetch the pot and some cups and let us chat for a bit."

Moments later Miranda turned to her uncle. "What ever has happened? Is the viscount unhappy with the house?" she asked as she poured a cup of tea for her uncle.

"No, my pet. Nothing like that. It is just that his lordship expressed a wish to have a chat with you about the house. It was for that very purpose I proposed I join him. All the way in to town he only wished to speak about you, my dear—how we happened to bring you up; you know; that sort of thing—and I was sure that he had every intention

231

of discussing how you were going to proceed with the house. But you saw him! I had no need of his fetching me back to the office. Now my carriage is all the way back at Farnsfield and someone will be put to the trouble of bringing it to the city. Truly, I do not understand the man."

Miranda frowned as she tried to come to an understanding of his lordship's strange behavior. She gave it up with a shake of the head. "Do you think I ought to go out to Farnsfield with you tomorrow?"

"Perhaps, perhaps. I shall have to think about it. In the meantime, I have to worry about my carriage. Will they know to bring it here, or do you think they will stop at Basford?"

Lord Farnsworth was just as surprised at his action as Thorpe had been. In fact, one might have guessed that he was even more upset, for he urged his horses on and raced out of town in a manner most unusual for him. It was not until he had put a mile or two between himself and Nottingham that he slowed his beasts to a walk and began to think.

He had come all the way to Nottingham to speak with Miss Miranda, just especially to speak with her—and he had not! Instead, he had slipped out of Thorpe's office feeling strangely guilty, so much so that he had had to get away and quickly.

What was he thinking about at that moment? It was not about what but about whom! Devil take the girl! What was there he had to say to her that was so important it could not wait? Not a thing! Then why in heaven's name had he made such an ass of himself by rushing in to Nottingham?

He truly could not say. He recalled how pleased he had been to know that she would be at Farnsfield and how disappointed he had felt upon learning that she was working in Thorpe's office instead. Of course, that was why he had had to come to the city. But then, why had he held so brief a conversation? Obviously because he had nothing to say to her!

He hauled back on the reins, bringing his curricle to a halt, and shook his head. No, that was not it. He had had a strong wish to pass the time of day with Miranda, and it had dawned upon him that such behavior on his part would have been most exceptional. He hardly knew the girl!

Yes, she was a very nice girl. She was, in truth, rather charming—and quite pretty, too. He had been attracted to her from the very first, now that he came to think of it. Actually, if he had not been head over heels in love with Lady Katherine . . . an architect's niece? The entire business just did not bear thinking on! She was to build him a house, and that was all there was to it. But even that was odd. It was he who ought to be building a house for her, dammitall! Why could he not have gotten himself an architect who was an ordinary chap and not a female?

He certainly had tried.

He shook his head again, flipped the reins, and started off for Winkwood at a brisk trot. He had not had a thing to eat all day, and it was getting on to three in the afternoon. By God, he was hungry!

At dinner that night Sir Toby informed him that Lady Katherine was expecting his lordship to escort her to see the new building. For his part, the squire went on, it was bound to be a dreadful bore and he was going to attend a cricket match to be played on Hucknall Common.

This news did not set well with his lordship. He did not want to go over to Farnsfield for a while. His strange experience still occupied his thoughts, and he wanted an opportunity to lay it to rest before he met with the Thorpes again.

He wrote to Lady Katherine, informing her that pressing business demands would fully occupy his time for the next week, but that he would be happy to escort her to the construction site one week from that day.

CHAPTER XIX

Since Lady Katherine was more interested in the designer of the building than in the building itself, she was disappointed to learn from Tony one week later that Miranda would not be found at the site. She hid her disappointment well, so that during the short ride from Hexgreave to Farnsfield, Tony found her enthusiasm high.

The weather was inclement with an overcast sky and a damp ground, the air being filled with a fine drizzle that made everything clammy to the touch. Neither Tony nor Katherine was happy to have to go about in it.

When they arrived at Farnsfield, they noticed at once that the house now had a completed look. The roof had been finished, at least to the extent that the final shape of the building could be realized. Apparently Nicolson was driving his men like fury to get the work done, so that he could be free to begin other assignments that were being held up.

Before the house a canvas canopy had been hung, beneath which Tony and Katherine discovered Mr. Thorpe and Miranda busily at work upon a large deal table. Although it was dry under this temporary shelter, there was no heat and it was little more comfortable than under the open sky. Lady Katherine was unhappy on that account, but even more so to find Miranda there after having been assured by Tony that she was in Nottingham.

Tony, on the other hand, was quite pleased and accepted Miranda's invitation to go over the new drawings with her so that she might explain to him how the rooms were being laid out. Lady Katherine evinced a desire to see the interior of the building, out of need to find better shelter than the canopy, but she was informed by Mr. Thorpe that it would be neither safe nor instructive, as that was where the greatest activity was now going on.

The result was that her ladyship had to simulate an interest in what Miranda was saying and observe, with rising resentment, how Tony hung upon her every word. It was nothing like she had thought it would be, and her impatience to be gone mounted with every passing minute.

By the time Tony was satisfied that the house was indeed progressing to a happy conclusion, some forty minutes had passed, and Lady Katherine's teeth were beginning to chatter.

Miranda, happening to glance up, noted how unhappy the lady looked. "Lord Farnsworth," she remarked, "I do believe that Lady Katherine is not dressed appropriately for this occasion. Unfor-

236

tunately, there is no warm, dry place available for her here."

Tony looked up in surprise. "You are not really uncomfortable, are you, Katherine?" he asked.

"Y-yes, I am!" she stammered, hugging her wrap more tightly about her.

"Oh, I say, you ought to have said something! In that case, we shall have to be off. My thanks to you, Miss Miranda. I am inordinately pleased with the work, and you may inform Mr. Nicolson that his speed in rushing the house to completion will be duly appreciated."

He then escorted Lady Katherine back to his carriage and drove off with her.

"Really, Tony, did you have to spend so much time with that female?" demanded Lady Katherine. "One could see at a glance that the place was almost done. There was not the slightest need to put your head together with hers for so long and in so public a place. To tell the truth, I felt quite neglected."

"I assure you I did not put my head together with hers, as you put it, for any purpose but the business in hand. That she is a woman I do not hesitate to admit, but it so happens that she is all that we have got for an architect in this case. If I am to confer with my architect, it is incumbent that I put my head together with Miss Miranda's. Surely you can understand that."

"All I understand is I am freezing and there is

not all that much to divert one at the site of a building being erected. I should not even care if we were attending the construction of Buckingham Palace. If they did not provide the minimum of comfort, they need not bother with the palace as far as I am concerned."

"I say, Katherine, it may not be Buckingham Palace, but it will be my home and my seat. It is where I intend to dwell. I must be sure that all is being done in accordance with my wishes."

"Oh, Tony, did we not have great fun in London? Surely you do not plan to renounce London so that you may rot away in the wilds of Nottingham. Let Farnsfield be your seat. That does not mean you actually have to *live* there."

Tony drew up on the reins and brought his vehicle to a halt before he turned to her. "I do not understand you, Katherine," he said. "I was assured that you liked the place and assumed that—er—you would not find such a dwelling exceptional."

"I do not find it exceptional. It is a most proper little place for a viscount to number amongst his holdings, but if he is to amount to anything in the fashionable world, it is in London he must do so. Surely you will be leasing a town house there for the season each year, will you not?"

Tony laughed hollowly. "I could easily afford to, but where's the point? My wealth is derived from the productivity of my land, not from the mere fact that I own it. This calls for my constant attention and therefore my presence. Katherine, that little house is being raised upon the spot that was my home, so that it, too, will be my home."

Lady Katherine shrugged her shoulders. "So that means you have got to go out to Farnsfield every day to see this female. I thought you said she would not be there."

"That was my understanding. If you had been listening, you would have heard her explain that she had come out because her uncle was under the impression that I wished to speak with her."

"How very obliging, I must say. Shades of Caesar and his harem!"

"I beg to inform you that the Romans did not have harems, my lady," Tony retorted coldly.

"Somebody had harems and, besides, that is not the point and you know it! Pray inform me, my lord, what is it you see in that female—female architect?"

Tony stared at her, puzzled and frustrated. Something was quite wrong, and he did not know what he could say to mend matters with her.

"It is very cold and I wish to go home," she said. "Kindly proceed, my Lord Farnsworth."

"Yes, of course," said Tony as he started up the carriage. "Katherine, I do not know what has come over you, but you are marvelously changed suddenly."

"I do not care to discuss the matter, my lord. Please take me home."

They said not another word until they were at the front portal of Hexgreave. He helped her out of the curricle and she took her leave of him, pointedly neglecting to invite him inside. If he, too, had not felt chilled before this, he did so now.

With relations between himself and Lady Katherine under strain and his host, Sir Toby, being less than sympathetic, Tony began to visit the construction site every day. Each time he passed Hexgreave, he felt troubled and looked to see if Lady Katherine could be discerned upon the grounds. She never was, but the small anguish he experienced passed quickly as his new house came into sight.

He was becoming more than pleased with it and was now permitted to enter the building. Mr. Thorpe acted as his guide and tried to explain the arrangements. A few such tours and Tony gave vent to his dissatisfaction by asking carping questions of Mr. Thorpe, so that the gentleman was forced to arrange to have Miranda come out again. From that time on, with her at the site every day, his lordship found everything very much to his satisfaction and began to spend more and more of his time in her company, until she had to protest.

"My lord, I appreciate the depth of your interest in the work, but I must point out that when I am with you, I am not at my table. There are still quite a number of details that have to be worked out, and you are keeping me from my plans. It will not be long before Mr. Nicolson will be at me for them."

"I beg your pardon, Miss Miranda. Of course, you are right," he agreed. From then on he kept her only a half-hour each day.

Days later, when the house was approaching completion, Miranda let out a sigh and put down the pencil she had been using to point out to Tony the last touches to be executed.

"Are you in some way not satisfied, Miranda?" he asked.

She looked up at him and smiled. "Oh no, Tony. I could not be more pleased. The house is precisely what I envisioned. It is just that it is almost over, and I hate to see it come to an end."

"Aye, it has turned out to be a bit of fun in the end—but, I say, once it is done I am sure you will gain the greatest pleasure going through all of its chambers and seeing everything precisely as you imagined it."

"I fear not, Tony. It is a house that I love now, but then it will be someone else's. I am not cut out to be an architect. I should want to possess every house I planned."

Tony laughed. "In that case, you will require a very wealthy husband to support your hobby-horse."

Miranda laughed. "I think it will be easier to forgo the pleasure."

"What, of getting married?"

"No, you idiot, of building houses," she retorted, laughing.

His laughter joined with hers, and for a moment they looked at each other.

Her eyes dropped and she turned away to stare at the house. Tony came to stand beside her, and for a moment they both were silent.

"It is a lovely house, my dear, and I thank you for it from the bottom of my heart," he finally said. "When I think of the monstrosity your uncle wished to saddle me with, I thank the Lord for you!"

"Oh, Tony!" she cried without looking at him. Then she snatched up a handkerchief to her eyes and rushed away to disappear under the canopy.

Tony was startled. He made a move to follow her, and then thought better of it. Slowly he made his way back to his curricle and, as he drove off, there was a very thoughtful expression on his face.

He did not visit Farnsfield for the next few days, nor did he pay his respects at Hexgreave. On Saturday he received two notes. There was one from Countess Lovelace inviting him to join the family for dinner on the morrow after church. He put it aside thoughtfully and picked up the other.

It was from Mr. Thorpe announcing that the work was completed and that only his approval was needed for him to take possession of his new house.

He set that note down beside the other and stared at the two of them for half an hour.

Sunday morning the sun had just risen when the front door of Winkwood House opened and Lord Farnsworth came striding out. He went down to the stable and ordered a sleepy-eyed groom to saddle up his horse, walking back and forth and slapping at his boot top with his crop impatiently as his wishes were being carried out.

With the horse saddled, he mounted and rode off at a canter towards Farnsfield.

The site was now deserted. Even the canopy had been struck, leaving the entire vista dominated solely by the new house. It sat there, a light-gray, many-windowed palace, the scarred, brown, unfinished landscape about it putting him in mind of a lovely lady who, dressed to the nines, had muddied her skirts. He smiled and then dismounted.

Entering the place, the odor of drying plaster and paint assailed his nostrils, and he began to wander through the rooms, recalling in each one

Miranda's comments. But even as it had been then, he could not see the place through her eyes. Each chamber was just a barren expanse to him, and his displeasure mounted with every room into which he ventured. It was quite obvious that, if the place were ever to become a home for him, it needed something more. He snorted, turned on his heel, and strode out of the house.

CHAPTER XX

"Now I hope you are satisfied, young lady! You have managed to make of yourself quite a cake in the neighborhood!" declared Mrs. Thorpe. "Of course, you know what they are saying. It was never a house you were after building but a viscount you were after marrying."

"Oh, Aunt Martha, it makes no difference to me. I have had the pleasure of building my own house, just as I had envisioned it."

"Your own house indeed! I shall tell you whose house it will be. It will be Lady Katherine's house. Everyone knows she has set her cap for his lordship. Really, Miranda, I always thought that you were a sensible young lady."

"I assure you, it was not the viscount I was after but the house. It could have been a duke's or a merchant's; still I should have done it."

"Better it had been a merchant's, my dear. Then, at least, you would have had some chance of winning the fellow." She turned to the maid who had just entered the sitting room. "Oh, yes, Clara, what is it?"

"It is the Viscount Farnsworth come to call, Mum. What shall I say to him?"

"Indeed, I was sure I had heard the door—the *viscount*, did you say? Well, show the gentleman in! And quickly, you stupid girl! Wait! The parlor! Show him into the parlor—and offer him a chair!"

The maid slipped away.

"Merciful heavens! What business has he to call upon us of a Sunday?" Aunt Martha continued. "Do you see what comes of having dealings with viscounts? Where is your uncle? He has come to see Sylvester! Where is that fool of a man?"

"Aunt Martha, there is naught to be agitated about. Uncle Sylvester went to visit Mr. Adams. It is quite all right. I am sure I can respond to any of the viscount's questions. Here, let me straighten your kerchief."

As she did so, Mrs. Thorpe moaned, "A viscount come to call on a Sunday and I looking like a bedraggled cat! What ever will he think?"

"Nothing at all, I assure you. He has come about the house. I am quite sure he has no designs upon you, dear aunt."

"Oh, go 'way with you!" smirked Mrs. Thorpe, giving Miranda a gentle shove.

"Good morning, ladies. It is kind of you to receive me," said Tony, turning from the hearth to greet them.

"You are most welcome, my lord," returned

Mrs. Thorpe. "Would you care for some tea and cakes?"

"No thank you, Mrs. Thorpe. I know it is Sunday, but I come upon the business of my house."

"Ah, Lord Farnsworth," said Miranda, "my uncle is away from home at the moment, but I should be most willing to answer your complaints, if that is what it is. In the event I cannot, I can fetch my uncle. He is not but ten minutes away at a neighbor's."

"No, that will not be necessary. It is the architect I wish to speak with. Perhaps you will be kind enough to oblige me with your company. We can talk my business over as we go for a stroll in the lane."

"In the sight of our neighbors, my lord—and on a Sunday?" exclaimed Mrs. Thorpe. "What will they think?"

"Surely, Aunt Martha, I am old enough to be seen with a gentleman who, as everyone knows, has business with Uncle Sylvester and myself."

"Mrs. Thorpe, I pray you will set your mind at ease," added Lord Farnsworth. "I shall take very special care of your niece, rest assured. I cannot complete my home without her."

His charming smile quite routed both Mrs. Thorpe's wits and her objections.

As they came out onto the lane, Miranda declared, "Tony, I do not see how I can do any more with the house. My work is completed and it now stands just as I always saw it. Do you wish something changed? Then you must speak with Uncle Sylvester. I am not at all competent for that."

"Yes, I do intend to, but first I must confer with you, my dear."

"Very well."

"I went over to inspect the house this morning—"

"My, but you are an early riser!"

"Miranda, I pray you will listen and not give vent to pointless remarks."

"Yes, Tony."

"By the way, I never thought to ask. Do you have any objections to walking with me?"

"Not at all, Tony."

"Good. I do not have any objections to walking with you. As a matter of fact, I have never forgotten that stroll we took out of Nottingham."

"Neither have I, Tony."

"Good. Well, my objection to the house as it stands is—"

"Oh no, Tony! It is such a perfect house!"

"Miranda, I did not say that I objected to the house. Yes, I do agree it is a perfect house, but it lacks something inside. I mean to say, when you were taking me through it, you made each chamber come alive, as it were. Now I have been back, and to me each chamber is just so much space, bounded by walls. The place needs proper furniture and draperies and all manner of decoration. I should want it just as you have always seen it. Can you do that for me?"

Miranda came to a stop and looked up at him with pain in her eyes. "Tony, I take as a compliment your faith in my taste, but it is a brand-new house and the news is all about that you will be tying the knot with Lady Katherine. Surely you must grant the new Viscountess Farnsworth the prerogative of decorating the place."

Tony looked a bit taken aback but pleasantly so, for he was smiling. "I never thought of that!" he exclaimed. "But of course! My dear Miranda, will you do me the honor of decorating my house?"

"But Tony, did I not just finish telling you . . ." Her voice trailed away as she remained staring up into his face. "T-Tony, d-do you know what you are saying?" she stammered, her eyes searching his for the confirmation she desperately desired.

For an answer his arms came up about her and he pressed her close to him as he brought his lips down upon hers in a demanding kiss.

In the midst of the overwhelming passion that gripped her as she clung to Tony, there came to Miranda the realization that they were out upon a public thoroughfare. In great confusion she broke away and exclaimed, "Tony, everyone can see us!"

As he reached out for her again, he said, "Indeed, now your reputation will be all to tatters unless you marry me. For who ever heard of a gentleman kissing his architect to any good purpose?"

It was some months later that Mr. Sutcliffe, snug in his office in London, came across an item in the society gazette announcing the wedding of Anthony Viscount Farnsworth to Miss Miranda Thorpe.

He sniffed and muttered to himself. "Yes, that is it, by heaven! I always suspected that those hen-tracked drawings were a bit of a farce. Female architect, indeed!"

Love—the way you want it!

Candlelight Romances

MADELEINE A. POLLAND

SABRINA

Beautiful Sabrina was only 15 when her blue eyes first met the dark, dashing gaze of Gerrard Moynihan and she fell madly in love—unaware that she was already promised to the church.

As the Great War and the struggle for independence convulsed all Ireland, Sabrina also did battle. She rose from crushing defeat to shatter the iron bonds of tradition . . . to leap the convent walls and seize love—triumphant, enduring love—in a world that could never be the same.

A Dell Book $2.50   (17633-6)

Once you've tasted joy and passion, do you dare dream of

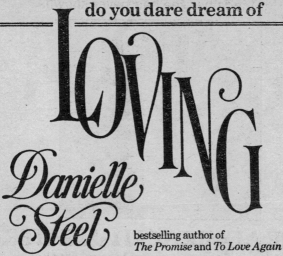

LOVING
Danielle Steel

bestselling author of
The Promise and *To Love Again*

Bettina Daniels lived in a gilded world—pampered, adored, ador-
ing. She had youth, beauty and a glamorous life that circled the
globe—everything her father's love, fame and money could buy.
Suddenly, Justin Daniels was gone. Bettina stood alone before a
mountain of debts and a world of strangers—men who promised
her many things, who tempted her with words of love. But
Bettina had to live her own life, seize her own dreams and take
her own chances. But could she pay the bittersweet price?

A Dell Book == **$2.75 (14684-4)**